HOLIDAY TREASURE

Billionaire Bachelors: Book Ten

By Melody Anne

COPYRIGHT

© 2014 Melody Anne

Printed and published in the United States of America.

Published by Gossamer Publishing Company

Editing by Nicole and Alison

DEDICATION

This is dedicated to the Eugene Mission, which takes in those who are homeless and provides warm beds and nourishing food. There are many places like this all over the country, and many people have gotten a second chance because of them.

NOTE FROM THE AUTHOR

I LOVE THE holiday season, love all the decorations, and especially love the happiness that's in abundance as families come together. I wanted to write a short, sweet romance about the way a single event can change the way you think and feel about others and yourself, and that's how *Holiday Treasure* began.

This holiday season, remember that many people are so much less fortunate than you, and that the holidays are a difficult time of year for them. You can make a child smile by picking up a gift from one of the giving trees at stores like Walmart, Shopko and Target. It costs only a few dollars, yet it can bring joy for years to come.

I lived a couple of years in the foster-care system, and I know well that receiving a special gift stays with you forever. My fondest gift was a Cabbage Patch Doll that Santa brought me on Christmas Eve when I was about seven years old. I have it to this day.

Merry Christmas to you all. May your holidays be filled with love, laughter and family!

Melody Anne

BOOKS BY MELODY ANNE

BILLIONAIRE BACHELORS

*The Billionaire Wins the Game

*The Billionaire's Dance

*The Billionaire Falls

*The Billionaire's Marriage Proposal

*Blackmailing the Billionaire

*Runaway Heiress

*The Billionaire's Final Stand

*Unexpected Treasure

*Hidden Treasure

*Holiday Treasure

BABY FOR THE BILLIONAIRE

+The Tycoon's Revenge

+The Tycoon's Vacation

+The Tycoon's Proposal

+The Tycoon's Secret

+The Lost Tycoon

RISE OF THE DARK ANGEL

-Midnight Fire – Rise of the Dark Angel – Book One

-Midnight Moon – Rise of the Dark Angel – Book Two

-Midnight Storm – Rise of the Dark Angel – Book Three

-Midnight Eclipse – Rise of the Dark Angel – Book Four
– **Coming Soon**

SURRENDER

=Surrender – Book One

=Submit – Book Two

=Seduced – Book Three

=Scorched – Book Four

FORBIDDEN SERIES

+Bound – Book One

+Broken – Book Two – **December 15th 2014**

HEROES SERIES

-Safe in his arms – Novella – Baby it's Cold Outside Anthology-**October 2014**

-Her Unexpected Hero – Book One – **Releases Feb 28th 2015**

-Who I am with you – Novella – **Coming soon**

-Her Hometown Hero – Book Two – **Releases June 2015**

PROLOGUE

TANNER STORM LEANED back comfortably in his chair as his sister, Brielle, vented her wrath and her frustration.

"How are you so damn calm, Tanner?" she shouted as she paced back and forth in the front room of his plush penthouse. "The old man has ripped everything from us! Everything!"

"He can't take what he doesn't know about," Tanner said, not fazed the least.

"What are you talking about? He froze all of my assets, my cards, everything. He stopped my payments on bills. I will be homeless soon and he doesn't even care. If I don't play his stupid little game, then I am screwed."

What neither his father nor his siblings knew was that Tanner had his own wealth. He hadn't been close to his family in a very long time, and he hadn't wasted all his time away. He'd taken a different path than any of them, and he'd managed to make some incredibly good investments. But he didn't want any of them to know.

Yes, he could help his sister out, but for some odd reason, he wasn't sure he wanted to. Sure, their dad's little lesson — to teach them all how to be responsible — was pretty laughable, and Tanner knew it, but unless he wanted his family to find out everything, what could he do but play along when the old man decided to put on his puppet show?

When he'd received the offer for the building from his father as a test to see whether he was worthy to be reinstated as an heir to the old guy's empire, he'd thought it nothing but a joke — a very annoying joke — but a joke nonetheless, with no laughs anywhere in sight. But no, it was right there in black and white on his father's letterhead.

One part of Tanner wanted to play the game, wanted to take one of his father's projects and make it succeed. It would prove to the old man that Tanner was not someone to write off so easily. Another part of him wanted to tell his father to stick it where the sun didn't shine.

Ah, he still hadn't made up his mind. How was he to follow his dad's terms and make a go of the stupid place? But when he'd checked out the property, he couldn't help but grow excited. Even now, brick and mortar could make a rational man see dollar signs.

Looking at his sister, a woman of beauty and intelligence, and someone he'd once thought the sun rose and fell upon, made him even more determined to prove their father wrong. Somewhere along the way, his family had fallen apart.

Was his father doing a good thing? No. Tanner wouldn't take it that far. But still…

He tuned back in, and his sister's ranting helped Tanner make his decision. He would accept his father's project, dammit. He would take the failing apartment complex his father had bought and he would rip it down and put in its place something so beautiful, so amazing, so profitable, that his father would have to admit he'd been wrong about his son.

He suddenly wanted to get started. This project was stirring his blood, exciting him. It would be a lot of fun, and fun wasn't something he'd had in a long time.

"Brielle," he said with sudden determination, "you can pace and cry all you want, but the bottom line is that you either accept this or not. We might not always like what is thrown our way, but our character is defined by the decisions we make." He stood up and moved toward the door with a gesture whose meaning was clear — follow me and get out.

He was fed up with his sister's tantrum, and he really didn't want to deal with her any longer.

"You're a jerk, Tanner. You always have been and always will be," she said, grabbing her purse and following him.

"Sorry, sweetheart, but I just don't…care."

His smile, if you could call it that, made his sister glare at him before she walked out his door.

As he shut it, the smile fell away. Yes, he *was* a jerk,

someone who pushed anyone and everyone away from him. But wasn't that the way he wanted to be? It sure as hell made his life more comfortable and efficient. Yes, he was managing quite well, he told himself as he went toward his study.

He had a project to head, and he wasn't going to waste any more time. Once Tanner Storm set his mind to something, he didn't stop until it was finished.

CHAPTER ONE

MR. STORM, YOU may think that you're above the law, but I guarantee you that you are not! This is the fourth time I've seen you in my courtroom in the last three months. It's become a bad habit, one that I don't appreciate. I don't care how much you're paying your group of attorneys. It's not getting you out of trouble this time."

"Your Honor—"

The judge did not take kindly to Tanner Storm's interruption. "Do not make me add contempt of court to your list of crimes," Judge Kragle said. "The conditions of your building are deplorable. I'm absolutely appalled that you'd leave women and children with no working elevators, with corroding pipes, and *with no heat*. I've thought long and hard about your punishment—"

"Your Honor," Tanner's attorney broke in, "Mr. Storm

has been trying to get the building condemned since he took ownership six months ago. If the tenants would take his incredibly generous offer to vacate, they could relocate to a much safer environment for their families, and he could tear the building down and start the project he has made plans for already."

"Mr. Henry, sit down," the judge said. "I've read through the files — I'm not blind. Mr. Storm has made it more than clear that he looks down his nose at this building, which he seemed to receive as a consolation prize in some family game of inheritances and trust funds. Don't insult my intelligence by telling me that Mr. Storm has these people's best interests at heart. The complex that he plans to build wouldn't be even *marginally* affordable to the current tenants, who are struggling to make ends meet *without* having the added pressure of moving." Judge Kragle's voice was quiet but stern, especially when he wanted to emphasize any of his remarks.

Tanner's first attorney obediently sat down, but another one rose in his place.

"You may not like our client, Your Honor, but he's well within his legal rights," said this attorney, a well-known shark, his demeanor confident, his suit costing more than most people paid for a car.

"No, Mr. Silt, he most certainly is *not* obeying the law. If you've managed to forget, the jury has already rendered its verdict, and not in your client's favor. We are now in the *sentencing* phase — remember that? — *and* I've made my decision. Tanner Storm, please rise," the judge said, a smile of pure satisfaction on his face that made Tanner more than a bit nervous, and nerves weren't usually part of his psychic makeup. "It seems that you haven't learned from your previous experiences standing before me, so I've decided to try a different penalty. You'll spend three days in jail, beginning immediately after I've finished here."

There was a murmur in the courtroom, everyone shocked that Judge Kragle would dare send Tanner Storm, the son of a billionaire, to jail. Tanner just smiled. He'd be out in six hours, max. He had nothing to worry about.

"After your jail sentence, you'll be under house arrest in the same building your tenants are living in. You will live there for twenty-four days, starting the first day of December, and ending on Christmas Day, December Twenty-Fifth."

The judge paused, and Tanner's eyes widened in shock. He felt his first stirrings of real unease. There was no way that he could stay in that building for such an extended time. It didn't even have Internet access. How was he supposed to get anything done?

"Furthermore, you aren't allowed to do any updates, additions, construction, repairs, or alterations on your own apartment that you don't provide for the rest of the building first," the judge continued. "If you want to bring the comforts of home to the complex, be my guest, but *your* unit will be the last to be worked on. The conditions of the building are appalling, and it would do you some good to learn a bit of humility. Your father is a good man, a man who is obviously trying to teach you much needed respect for those around you. He has served this community well since moving here, and he has given you this opportunity in the hopes that you will do the right thing."

"But—" Tanner was getting desperate.

"I'm not finished! You will also be required to serve one hundred and twenty hours of community service during your time."

"I can't serve all those hours and still do my job," Tanner burst out, fury overcoming his usual discretion.

"I guess you'll have to take time off from work, Mr. Storm. You will serve every single hour or I'll impose the full sentence allowed by law — five years in a state prison."

Judge Kragle sat back and looked Tanner in the eye. Tanner attempted to exude confidence, but the set of his incredibly high-priced attorneys' shoulders told him more than anything that he just wasn't getting out of this.

"Do I need to scrub some graffiti off ghetto walls?" Tanner made no attempt to hide his sarcasm. He had donated astronomical amounts of money to charity in his life; his time, however, was priceless, and he wasn't happy about having to share it — to waste it, probably.

"No, Mr. Storm. You'll be volunteering as Santa Claus this season."

Tanner stared back in horror as the judge banged his gavel and the courtroom erupted. Reporters tried in vain to get a statement from him as — the grossest indignity of all — he was handcuffed and led away through a back door.

Merry freaking Christmas to him!

CHAPTER TWO

TANNER GROUND HIS teeth while he packed a bag. Nope. Wouldn't need his hand-tailored suits. Nope. Wouldn't need his Rolex. Nope. Wouldn't need anything he had in his penthouse on top of a luxury high-rise in downtown Seattle.

Anything he took with him to his temporary prison would stay behind when he left. He wouldn't want to bring back the filth he was sure was going to seep into his very bones while he stayed in that wretched building for three long weeks and change.

He'd fought the judge's orders — paid a lot of his own money to his useless attorneys to get him out of this ridiculous sentence. They'd been sweating as they told him they couldn't get the judge's ruling overturned. Tanner delivered a savage kick to his newly bought duffel bag, which had the misfortune to be lying in his path.

"Are you almost ready, Mr. Storm?"

Tanner nearly growled at the two officers waiting in his doorway. He hadn't even been allowed to come back to his penthouse without escorts. No. They thought he might be a flight risk. Damn right he was a flight risk.

They'd slapped some ridiculous contraption on his ankle as if he were a real criminal, and they were hauling him by police car to the apartment building in what had been one of the less affluent parts of the city.

Still, over the past decade, the city *had* vastly improved the area near where the building was located, and the site was ideal for a profitable project. With Tanner designing and building, the area would be brand new and his bank account would grow even fatter.

But nothing had gone right since he'd taken over the damned place. He'd been trying to buy off the tenants, get them to leave, and get going on demolition, but only half the people had taken his more than generous offer. The remaining tenants flatly refused to budge.

His legal team hadn't found any loopholes yet, so he'd left it to his very efficient business crew to help out. He hadn't *known* the heat in the building had been turned off, and if he'd been aware of his employees' plans, he would have called an immediate halt. He wasn't a monster. Not that the judge had let him get that far in his explanations.

"Not yet," Tanner finally snapped at the officers. Their impatience was becoming almost palpable as he took his sweet time.

Tanner was beginning to think that proving his father wrong just wasn't worth it. But he'd already started down this path and he certainly wouldn't be called a quitter. No, he'd pretend to be a party his father's scheme for family reunification — for now. But only because he saw the potential to add to his own portfolio. He'd construct a new complex in place of the monstrosity his father had given him. Piece of cake, piece of lucrative cake. He just had to get the stupid tenants to vacate first.

Because his father had put certain annoying clauses in the contract, Tanner couldn't force the people out; all he could do was offer them generous moving packages. Why did everything have to be so difficult? He should tell his father to kiss off and just walk away from the whole project. And it would have been so easy to do that. Why did the though turn his stomach?

Okay, okay. He loved his family, even if they'd run into a few speed bumps over the years.

Crew was now married and in love, happier than Tanner had ever seen him. Well, that was good for his brother, but none of that was in the cards for him. He was just trying to make an honest buck — well, an honest billion bucks — and between his father and this freaking Judge Kragle, he was hitting walls left and right.

Tanner searched for the running shoes his assistant had picked up for him. He'd sent the man out to buy all new clothes from a local mall. When Tanner was down at those decaying apartments, he didn't want to be tabloid fodder.

Hell, he didn't know how to shop, hadn't done it, well, ever that he could remember. Yes, he'd shopped with short-term girlfriends in some high-end malls on the banks of the Seine, but he'd never once entered a middle-class mall, or any mall, in America.

Wearing the scratchy jail clothes for the last three days had been seriously unpleasant, and he was determined to ban the color orange from his sight. But how much better were things now? For three weeks, or more accurately, twenty-four painful days, he was going to be stuck in denim and cotton, and even worse.

Polyester.

Tomorrow he had to put on a flipping Santa costume. Just the thought made his head itch. Who knows how many sweaty bodies had been in the same suit? He'd insisted that his assistant have it professionally cleaned. At least the senile judge had allowed him that much.

The man obviously needed to retire. It was long overdue and the judge looked like freaking Santa Claus himself. Maybe Judge Kragle should be the one down at the mall letting a bunch of sticky, snot-nosed brats climb all over *him*.

"Let's go," one of the officers said, this time not as pleasantly.

Tanner had dragged his feet long enough. If he didn't walk with them willingly, the fuzz were going to throw the handcuffs back on him and escort him through the building in a far less dignified manner than by simply walking behind him.

This day just kept on getting better.

He'd at least managed to talk the officers into allowing him to leave through his private penthouse entrance. The last thing he wanted at his exclusive high-rise was for anyone, rich, poor, or in between, to see him being escorted off to the cheap streets by some of Seattle's finest.

Undignified? As if!

Stepping from his apartment, he gave a long-suffering sigh as he pushed the elevator button and moved inside.

"Don't you guys have more important things to do than escort a law-abiding citizen around?" Tanner asked.

One of the officers threw his a scornful glance. "Are you suggesting that we're slackers, *Mister* Tanner?"

"I would never think that," Tanner replied. "I was just saying that there are people out there who are *actually* committing crimes, and yet you're both here 'escorting' me when I've never broken the law in my life."

"I beg to differ, Mr. Storm," the other officer snapped. "My *mother* lives in your *new* apartment complex. Or your *old* one. I think that having you stay there is sweet justice. Maybe this Christmas you'll actually find a heart." The guy snickered despite himself.

"Didn't your mother tell you that I offered each tenant a large sum to move out?"

"I hate men like you, men who think they can solve all the world's problems by throwing their wallets around. My mom has been in that building for thirty-five years. She has friends there, history, and she doesn't want to leave. She just wants the heat and water to work correctly, and for rodents and bugs to not crawl all over everything she owns."

"That's the exact reason I want to condemn the building and start over," Tanner said. He couldn't hide his frustration.

"The building is solid, and it wouldn't take much to bring it up to code," the officer told him heatedly. "You just need to get your priorities straight."

Tanner didn't feel like saying anything else as the elevator doors opened and the three of them stepped out into the garage.

The police car was waiting for him. When he hit his head as they *helped* him inside, his lips compressed.

Three weeks. He just had to remember this would be for only three weeks.

CHAPTER THREE

AS TANNER FOUND himself traveling the streets of Seattle in the back of a smelly police cruiser, he decided he was done talking to anyone and everyone. When they arrived at what would be his home for more than the next three miserable weeks, he couldn't keep the disgusted look from his face as one the officers opened the back door and grinned — yes, it was the one whose mother lived in the building. Tanner didn't feel too protected right now, and he really wanted to point out to both officers that it was their job to *serve* and *protect*, wasn't it?

But this cop was enjoying the authority part of his job far too much for Tanner's liking — the guy looked like he was itching to use his club, or even his gun. He was probably another underpaid public servant who thought men like Tanner needed to be knocked down a peg or two. No respect for the people who ensured he had a job by paying so much in taxes. Or it seemed like a lot, anyway.

"Have a pleasant stay, Mr. Storm," the officer said before tipping his hat and leaving Tanner standing on the broken sidewalk.

Those cops weren't worried he'd run now. They'd find him instantly, thanks to the device on his damned ankle. Thank the heavens the thing wasn't too big and he could hide it with a thick pair of socks. His humiliation would be complete if anyone saw the depths to which he'd fallen.

Deciding his self-pity party had gone on long enough, Tanner pulled hard on the building's heavy front door, which desperately needed some lubricant on the hinges. He was grateful to see no one about as he began his trek down the hallway. He wasn't there to make friends, and he didn't feel like speaking to a single person. The only people he'd likely find living here willingly were the type for whom burning in hell seemed appropriate.

Tanner reached his apartment, and he was almost afraid to open the door. The hallways weren't cluttered, but the paint was peeling and there was a musty smell in the air as if there were leaks that no one had bothered to patch up. He was sure mold was running rampant throughout the place.

That had to be a health risk — wouldn't it allow him to have the building condemned? He hadn't even bothered looking through the reports from the inspection yet — he left that kind of thing to his employees. Maybe it was time he went through them himself, line by line. He did have a lot of extra time on his hands for most of the next month, even with all the hours he had to wear a Santa costume. All he knew for sure was that he wanted to tear the outdated building down and start fresh. It would certainly be a lot less hassle.

His legal team had quickly put the kibosh on the crap about historical value that local societies had spouted. Anyway, he couldn't care less if the crown moldings had been handcrafted by early settlers of the area.

He wanted new. He wanted modern.

Squaring his shoulders, Tanner stepped inside his "new" apartment and looked around. The size of the place surprised him. A large living room was separated by a breakfast bar from a decent-sized kitchen. The appliances were extremely outdated, but the apartment wasn't as filthy as he was expecting.

Huge windows opened out onto the grungy street, but Tanner saw potential for the neighborhood, especially since every area except his building was cleaned up. The riffraff living in the building ensured that this particular neighborhood remained sketchy, but he'd been told that respectable businesses would come back if this building was replaced. Nearby, a new complex was in line to be completed next year. Things were improving here, dammit.

But he had to think about the here and now. And it could be worse. Down a short hallway, he found a roomy bathroom, again with outdated fixtures, but still decently clean. Then there were two bedrooms — with ridiculously small closets.

Okay, maybe they weren't that small, but he was used to everything being larger than normal. That thought brought his first smile of the day. It quickly disappeared when he heard someone call out.

"Hello?"

Who in the world would be coming into his place uninvited? No one even knew he was here, not even his brothers and his sister. He hadn't wanted to tell anyone. If his siblings got word that he was being forced to don a Santa suit, they'd be first in line to point cameras directly at him.

His only consolation was that the judge hadn't listed where he was to do his community service when the reporters swarmed around him after the hearing was over. He didn't doubt that they'd figure it out, though. This would be too juicy a photo op for anyone in the media to pass up. He'd just keep his fingers crossed that it didn't happen.

Walking back out to the living room, he found a petite blonde with bright blue eyes looking at him, a welcoming smile on her face. Before he was able to say anything, she spoke.

"Your door was open so I thought I'd see who was in here. They've frozen any of the apartments from being rented, so…" Her meaning was loud and clear. She thought he was a vagrant who had found a warm place to sleep.

Jeez. She wasn't the brightest bulb on the Christmas tree to be confronting someone who could be a criminal.

He approached her. "I won't be here long," he replied, his manner stiff. "But I am living here for now. Do you always just walk into other people's homes?"

His unpleasant tone made her take a step back, and he had to give her a few points for at least being a bit nervous.

"Sorry about that, but like I said, your door was open and these apartments aren't being rented," she said, leaving it hanging in the air. When he said nothing, she continued. "How long are you staying?" She didn't look him in the eye this time, but instead looked around the empty room. Nothing in it except for one large duffel bag.

"That's undetermined right now," he told her. He'd learned never to give out too much information and he didn't care what this woman thought about him, so let her wonder how he'd managed to rent an unrentable apartment.

The woman looked at him with wide eyes and a wavering smile, but she still just stood there as if trying to determine whether she could trust him or not. What if he were a serial killer? Did she have no self-preservation instincts at all?

"I've lived here for two years. It's a great place if you can get past the mice," she said with a laugh. "At least there are a lot of storage areas."

"Mice?" Tanner looked around uneasily.

"Yeah, but I've named them, so I'm not so scared of the little critters anymore."

"Named them?" Tanner almost found it amusing that he kept repeating what she said. Almost.

"Yeah, you know, like in *Cinderella*. Or *A Little Princess* — but Melchisidec was a rat, and there's a difference, of course. I would say the Disney mice would help you unpack, but you don't have anything here. Were you making sure you liked the place first?"

Tanner realized that he hadn't ordered a bed, a couch, anything. He wasn't looking forward to being here, and he just hadn't thought that far ahead. Of course he would need some basics, even for only from now until Christmas. His assistant should have been on top of this. Maybe it was time to hire a new one.

"Everything will be delivered later today," Tanner said as he moved toward the door. Would this woman take the hint?

"Oh, that must be nice not having to move it yourself. I despise moving. It's so physically and emotionally exhausting and then you *always* lose something in the process — every single time, no matter how organized you are or how carefully you label the boxes."

"Yes, moving is unpleasant," Tanner said dryly. "Well, I have some phone calls to make…" He held open the door she'd blown past when entering his place *illegally*. He'd really begun to care about legality.

"I'm sorry. I'll leave you be. My name is Kyla, by the way, Kyla Ridgley." She walked right up to him and held out her hand.

Tanner looked at it for a moment as if he didn't know what to do, but then his manners kicked in and he held out his own hand. "Tanner," he offered, and nothing more.

"Well, it's great to meet you, Tanner," she said, and then her warm, slender hand was somehow clasped in his.

Tanner nearly took a step back when their fingers

touched. It felt like a spark had just ignited between the two of them.

"Um, great to meet you," Kyla almost gasped. She jerked her hand from his and dashed through the door.

When she slipped inside the apartment right across the hall from his and quickly closed the door behind her, Tanner stared for several moments at the space she'd been occupying.

Maybe his "jail" time had just become a lot more bearable. With a slight smile lifting the corners of his mouth, he picked up his phone to call his assistant.

Furniture was his first priority.

Then, he was going to find out a bit more about his new neighbor. A three-week fling might just make this situation a whole lot easier to swallow.

CHAPTER FOUR

KYLA LEANED AGAINST her door and took a deep breath. Normally, men didn't intimidate her. She'd grown up with a loving family, and had enjoyed high school and the first two years of college. She'd had a healthy dating life.

Then…boom.

Her picture-book world had fallen apart in the blink of an eye. On a family vacation, they'd all been driving down a mountain road after a fun day of snowboarding. And then their car had skidded on black ice.

She was the only survivor.

After a week in the hospital, she'd been released, with nowhere to go where she felt safe. After dropping out of school — she couldn't face anything or anyone — she'd found herself at this apartment, both her place of refuge and a spot where she hoped to heal someday.

She knew it wasn't her fault that her family was gone. But why was she the only one to live? Why wasn't it her mother, who did charity work, or her father, who made a difference in the world through his teaching? Why couldn't her brother have survived? He'd graduated from high school the previous June and planned to join the military after college. He'd have been an officer and a gentleman.

No, she'd been the one to survive. The only one who still didn't know what she wanted to do with her life. So now she found herself taking odd jobs, just trying to hang on, instead of really living.

She'd been left her parents' home when they'd passed, along with a substantial inheritance, but she couldn't find it in her heart to use the funds or to stay in that house. She hadn't been there since the accident. She was too afraid to face the memories of those empty rooms. Seeing her dad wrestling with her brother on the living room floor, hearing their laughter and her mother's sweet singing ringing in from the kitchen. They were such an old-fashioned family in many ways — more than half a century later, they'd somehow captured the best of the 1950s without the worst that went along with it.

Never again would she and her brother wake up on Christmas morning and rush downstairs to open the gifts her parents had so lovingly picked out. The realization that these memories would play continually and vividly in her mind, although she would never see her family again in real life, whatever that was, made it all too overwhelming to face.

Kyla shook off the thoughts. It had been months since she'd allowed such painful memories to intrude so forcefully, but with Christmas not much more than three weeks away, her family was front and center more than ever before.

After all, December 23rd was the day her life had been irrevocably changed, the day she'd lost her family and suddenly found herself an orphan. It didn't look as if she'd ever again be able to enjoy the holiday she had once cherished.

Kyla was trying to put herself out in the world again, trying to meet people. She wasn't interested in dating, but the odd tingling her new neighbor had inspired shocked her. He couldn't have touched her heart — it was encased in ice. But he'd still had some effect on her, and considering his standoffish behavior, that made no sense at all.

Maybe it was because he'd been so cold in the way he spoke, and then so very hot to the touch. No matter. She closed her eyes, took a breath, and then told herself she wouldn't think about her temporary neighbor again.

Heck, the current owner of this stupid mass of brick and mortar, whoever had taken it over wanted them all kicked out on the street. She really didn't know how long she was going to get to stay. The thought of moving, of leaving the place she'd chosen as somewhere to heal, was terrifying. She didn't want to leave yet. She just wasn't ready.

Kyla felt herself drawn to her kitchen. What was going on? She went there slowly and was surprised when for the first time in two years she found herself succumbing to the urge to bake. It was something she and her mother had always done together, since before Kyla could have been any use at all except in licking the bowls. They would spend all day in the kitchen, whipping up goodies for family, friends, and neighbors. It had been a tradition, one that had died the minute her mother's heart had stopped beating.

As Kyla set out the items needed to make cookies, she found herself singing Christmas hymns, feeling a measure of peace that she had feared she would never feel again.

Three hours later, she pulled out the last batch of gingerbread men — and women and children, of course — and looked at her covered counters. Tears sparkled in her eyes as she painted frosting faces on the ones that had cooled off. When she lifted one up and took a bite, a soft smile lit her face. It felt like her mom was right there beside her. Kyla closed her eyes to relish the warmth of the moment.

Reluctantly coming back to reality, Kyla whispered, "Merry Christmas, Mom," before putting everything away, turning off the lights in the room, and getting ready for bed. Tomorrow she had work to do at the mall.

For now she was going to get lost in a good book while she waited for the forgetfulness of sleep to take her away.

CHAPTER FIVE

S PECIAL DELIVERY."

Tanner stood at his door with his jaw locked and fire burning in his eyes. This was so not happening to him.

"What in the hell are you doing here?" he snapped.

"Is that any way to treat your relatives?"

His brother Ashton and a newfound cousin, Max Anderson, were standing at his door with big grins on their faces.

"I didn't tell anyone I was going to be here, so I don't know how in the hell you managed to track me down," he said, opening the door and letting them inside, though he wanted to slam it in their faces instead. There was no use in trying to keep them out now that they knew where he was stuck for the next few weeks.

"Wow! This place must really suck for you, big shot,"

Ashton said with a laugh.

"Damn! I've seen cardboard boxes that have more class," Max added.

"Okay, are you going to crack jokes the entire visit?" Tanner asked. "Or are you going to tell me how you found me here and what you want?" He was pacing the room, really irritated that he had nowhere to sit and no alcohol to drink.

"I talked to Dad and he told me about your current situation. You know I had to check it out for myself. Max happened to stop by as I was getting ready to leave, and he didn't want to miss out on all the fun either."

"I'm so glad you care so much, little brother," Tanner snarled.

"I'd say you got one of the crappier properties. Don't forget that you did choose it."

"I chose it because I was planning on ripping this wretched place down and then building something that would actually add value to this benighted neighborhood. But with Dad's clauses, I can't force the tenants out. I've upped their move-out bonuses by triple and they're still being stubborn fools. Then some cracked judge made me stay here to show me what it's like for people who have less than I have. He's the one who will be shown, because I don't cave under pressure."

"I don't know, Tanner. I think one night here would be hell, let alone three or four weeks. Plus, I can't wait to see you in a nice fat Santa suit." Ashton wasn't even trying to hide his mirth — his brother's predicament was a doozy!

"I'm going to kill him. Dad must have gloated about all this. Fess up — he told you both, didn't he?"

"Nope. I learned it from the media," Max said. "Your horrified expression said it all." Max moved to one of the windows and looked out.

"Great. The entire city knows."

"I don't think the entire population cares," Ashton pointed out before breaking out into another grin. "Just the reporters and those who would love to hang you by your toes and let rats nibble on your hair."

"It's always such a pleasure to talk to you, Ashton. Why I don't invite you over more often, I'll never know."

"You didn't invite me this time, but I came anyway."

Ashton had always had a good sense of humor, but he tended to be more thoughtless and self-absorbed than any of his siblings. He had no problem taking delight in Tanner's suffering, because he'd never truly experienced any of his own.

Until now. That was all changing with the little game their father was playing.

"How is your own project going?" Tanner asked as he went to the kitchen counter and pulled himself up. He needed to get off his feet.

Ashton lost the grin on his face. "I'm in too good a mood to even talk about that."

"Oh, I see. You can mock me all you want, but when it comes to you, the subject is closed."

"You may think you got the raw end of the deal, but I'm

not so sure about that. I don't know what Dad was thinking when he picked up all these businesses, but I don't see how in the hell I'm supposed to do anything with mine," Ashton huffed.

"Damn, I wish I'd known you guys so much sooner. You both sound like little kids throwing a tantrum right now."

Tanner turned toward Max. He'd been so focused on his brother that he'd forgotten his cousin was even there with them.

"You lucked out, Max. You got a great father. Ours is a pain in the ass."

"I happen to like Richard," Max said.

"That's because you've only known him a year."

"Well, I look forward to many more," Max replied. "Since you have no furniture and no beer, I think it's time we head out."

"Yeah. That's a great idea," Tanner told him, but he was surprised by the way his stomach dipped. He might be acting as if he didn't want them there, but once they left, he knew he'd be stuck in this hellhole with nothing to do and no one to talk to.

Fighting with his family members seemed much more appealing than being utterly alone. He would rather swallow razor blades than admit that out loud, though.

"Get out of here. I obviously have things to take care of."

His brother and cousin took off, and Tanner slumped down on the counter. It was time to make some phone calls, time to decide who he was going to fire.

CHAPTER SIX

TANNER STRETCHED LUXURIOUSLY before climbing from the surprisingly comfortable bed. When he'd called about the furniture, furious that his assistant hadn't thought about it, Randy had said that it was already arranged, and that everything should be there within the hour. Tanner felt more than a bit bad right now. Why had he yelled at the poor guy? Maybe it was time to give him a raise.

Damn. This wasn't like him at all. He'd gone from wanting to fire an employee to considering increasing the fellow's pay. That turnaround was surprising, to say the least. but he had to blame his rash decision-making on the ridiculous mess of a situation he was in. In short, not his fault.

After a quick shower, Tanner walked into his living room. His assistant had done well there, too, with comfortable pieces that didn't appear too out of place in this dump. Yes, the man was good, he had to admit. And when he opened his front door, he was happy to find the newspaper waiting for him, another point in his assistant's favor. He grabbed it and went to sit down.

While he read his paper and drank a cup of coffee, Tanner leaned back, thinking this wasn't going to be so bad. Yes, the apartment sucked, but he could get through his sentence.

It was under a month, after all.

Just as he stood up to grab his wallet and coat and head over to the mall, a mouse ran across the floor, less than a foot from where he was standing. Normally not a man who scared easily, Tanner found himself jumping back and fighting the urge to shout. The creature squeezed behind his kitchen counters and disappeared.

Snatching up his phone, he punched the buttons and pulled up his assistant's contact information. "Get the damn rodent company out here today, Randy; hell, get every pest-control company in the city out here. I want this building purged of all rodents, insects, and any other of vile things that infest places like this. If I see a single one when I get home tonight, find another job!"

He hung up before the guy could say anything. Tanner didn't care if it took every exterminator in the forty-eight contiguous states — he wasn't going another night sharing sleeping quarters with those disgusting creatures.

The thought made him think of his unusual neighbor. How in the world could she possibly name the damn things?

What was wrong with her?

After throwing a leery glance at his now fully stocked cupboards, he walked out of the apartment. If he was late to his Santa gig, he had a feeling the cops would be showing up with guns drawn.

He could almost forget about the leash on his ankle. Almost, but not quite.

Not paying attention to where he was walking, Tanner pushed through the front doors of the apartment complex and tripped. He tried to catch himself before hitting the cold, hard cement, but it was too late. With a raging fury, he found himself sprawled out on the ground, his new pair of jeans ripped at the knees.

After shaking off the shock of falling, he picked himself back up and then turned toward the door and looked at the entrance. The cement steps were cracked and uneven, an obvious hazard.

Wrath pouring through him, he lifted his phone again and barely managed to keep from yelling as he told his assistant to have a construction foreman meet him at the mall during his lunch break.

Yes, it would be humiliating having to meet with the contractor at a mall, but he wasn't going to have someone trip coming in or out of the building and then get sue-happy. If he'd fallen, he was sure others would follow. And it was all on his ass now. Just great.

It took him only a few minutes to reach the mall by taxi once he took care of business, and then Tanner found himself in a stuffy changing area with the ugly-as-sin Santa suit hanging before him. Eyeing it as if it were a snake about to strike — or maybe a rabid rat — he finally got up his courage and ran his fingers gingerly down the red fabric, then watched the white faux fur instantly pouf back out. He squeezed it now — take that! — and it still bounced back.

At least the suit didn't appear to be as scratchy as his jailhouse clothes. That was some consolation. Sure it was. After getting into the damnable thing, Tanner turned toward the mirror and looked at himself with a disgusted snort.

"You have *got* to be kidding me," he gasped in abject horror. But at least no one would recognize him. The freaking thing even came with bushy glue-on eyebrows.

The added padding around his body made him feel like a stuffed animal, and he probably looked like one, too. He was surprised the mall didn't insist that he wear blush for a hint of jolliness; he certainly didn't have any otherwise. He had one reason to be thankful; with the fluffy mustache and beard, he didn't have to worry about pretending to smile at his young tormentors.

He had nothing to smile about.

Lifting the phone to his ear, he waited impatiently for his lawyer to pick up. "Keep trying to get me out of this," Tanner snapped.

"We're working on it, sir," the man replied.

Tanner hung up and made his way grudgingly into the main part of the mall Just out the door, he found himself confronted by kids who were there shopping with their parents.

"Santa!" a horde of them cried; they tugged free of their parents' hands and rushed forward. Hell, he hadn't even made it to his "throne" yet, and he was already suffering an onslaught of grubby fingers.

"Ho, ho, ho," he bellowed a bit menacingly, and he kept on moving forward. This was community service and he would do his job — but nothing said he had to like it.

Tanner turned the corner and beheld his new prison, which was decked out with so many sparkling decorations, he knew he'd end up with a headache from the glare before the day was out.

His elves began lining the children up as he took his seat and tried to prepare himself for the next eight hours. This was going to be an excruciatingly long day.

"Hello, Santa. Are you ready for your first visitor?"

Tanner's head whipped around as he recognized that voice.

Once again, he found himself caught in the bold blue gaze of his neighbor in the slums. What was her name? Kyla! Wow, he was stunned that he remembered. She'd been wearing a baggy sweatshirt the night before; she now had on a little elf costume that did her body far more justice.

Taking his own sweet time, he looked at her from head to toe, appreciating all the nice curves the costume did nothing to hide with its short skirt and fitted elf top. Her chest was a bit smaller than he normally liked, but on her frame, those puppies worked perfectly, and the nice curve of her delicious behind had him practically drooling in his Santa beard. His idle thought of spending a few weeks with his neighbor warming his bed had just become a serious plan.

"Bring the children up," he said, his voice deep with instant lust. She paused and he knew she had no clue that he was the neighbor she had met the afternoon before. Why not have a bit of fun with her then and lighten up his day? "Do you want to sit on Santa's lap?" he asked, grinning widely enough that she could see his teeth through all the fake hair.

He expected some sarcastic reply, something to show she was irritated with the dirty old man hitting on her. What he got instead took his breath away.

She leaned in close so none of the children could hear. "I've always had a Santa fantasy," she practically purred, making his heart rate soar before she doused him in cold water. "Too bad you won't get to hear what it is." With that she smiled and walked away.

Mmm, the things he would do with his neighbor. His attitude improved tenfold. When the first kid landed a bit too hard on his lap, he didn't even growl.

"I want a Barbie doll, and her Dream House, and an iPod, and…" The kid went on and on until she ran out of breath.

Tanner looked toward the camera as the bulb flashed and he wondered if he would be blind by the end of the day. After giving the girl a pat on her head, Tanner handed her a coloring book and then took the next kid, and the next, and the next.

By hour six, Tanner wasn't feeling nearly as happy as when he'd first discovered his hot Santa's helper. By closing, he was downright pissy.

This was going to be a hellacious few weeks. Even though he got to enjoy the view of his enticing neighbor's backside, it didn't quite make up for ordeals like these.

CHAPTER SEVEN

KYLA FUMBLED IN her purse for her apartment key as she moved down the sidewalk toward the apartment building. Before she could look up, her legs tangled, and she felt herself falling forward as she heard someone let out an *oof*.

To her horror, Kyla found herself on the cold cement, on top of a small boy. Rolling quickly off him, she sat up and immediately reached out.

"Are you okay? I am so sorry," she gasped as her hands ran over his arms and legs.

"I'm fine," he said, though his wheezing told her that he'd had the breath knocked out of him. "My grandma needs help, though," he said, almost pleading, his eyes desperate.

"Where is she? What's the matter?" Kyla was instantly panicked. She didn't handle emergencies very well.

"This way." The boy grabbed her hand and began to pull

her down the sidewalk. Kyla held his little hand and had to rush to keep pace with him as he moved. When they reached the bus stop halfway down the block, she found a woman sitting on the bench with a couple of plastic grocery sacks beside her and her shoulders hunched down low.

Kyla bent down to the woman, worried about what she would find. "Ma'am, are you okay?"

The woman looked up, her brow wrinkled, her gray eyes tired, and her hands showing clear signs of rheumatoid arthritis. "Oh, sweetie, I'm just fine. I did some shopping and I'm trying to get up the energy to carry the bags inside. Billy here was obviously alarmed — he's such a good boy! — and he took off to find help before I could call him back. Thank you for bringing him to me. I worry when he wanders. He's only five years old."

"Let me help you with the bags. Billy found me and said you needed assistance."

"Oh, that's not your job, doll. I can do it. It just takes me a little bit longer these days." The woman spoke with determination, though her voice sounded so exhausted.

"I'd be hurt if you didn't let me help," Kyla told her, and she grabbed both bags with one hand, though they *were* definitely heavy. She then held out the other hand to help the woman up.

"You're too kind. I used to move around a lot easier, but old age, arthritis, and creaky bones are making it more difficult these days," she said with a small laugh. "When they say seventy-five is the new fifty-five, they're lying — at least when it comes to some of us."

"I have days like that myself," Kyla replied as she stood next to the woman and they began a slow walk back to the apartment building.

"I'm Vivian, by the way. What's your name?"

"I'm Kyla. I met your grandson right outside my apartment building. Do you and Billy live in the apartments on this street?"

"Yes. I've been here for years, but my little boy just came to live with me not too long ago."

Kyla wanted to ask how the woman had ended up with her grandson, but she'd heard the pain in Vivian's voice, and she could tell the story wouldn't be a pleasant one. In any case, she didn't want to be intrusive.

"I'm surprised I haven't run into you before now," Kyla said as they made it to the building and she pushed open the slow-groaning doors.

"I don't get out as much as I used to. I have someone who shops for me once a week, but Billy needed a few things, and the shopper won't come back for three more days, so we had no choice but to go to the store."

"Which apartment do you live in? Ground floor?" Kyla hoped so, since the elevators didn't work and she couldn't imagine that Vivian would able to climb the stairs without major effort.

"Yes, thankfully. I'm in one-sixteen."

"We're practically neighbors. I'm in one-twelve," Kyla said.

"I hope you'll come in for a cup of tea so I can thank you properly for helping me," Vivian said as she pulled out a key and inserted it in the lock of her door.

"I would love to," Kyla told her.

They stepped inside, and Kyla was impressed with the woman's small apartment. It was spotless, and pictures filled the walls and the end tables by the couch. Holding pride of place in the center of the living room wall was a large framed picture featuring a smiling Billy and what looked like his parents. She again wondered why he was living with his grandmother now, but she couldn't bear to ask.

"Oh, Billy, remember to pick up your toys, sweetie," Vivian said as she nearly tripped over a bright little fire engine.

Was tripping the name of the game in this place?

"I'm sorry, Grandma," Billy said, quickly grabbing the truck before he took it to what looked like his toy box.

"It's okay. I just don't want to fall over," Vivian told him before moving to the kitchen and filling her teakettle with water and setting it on the stove, then taking two cups down.

Once Kyla set the heavy bags on the counter, Billy began emptying them and putting everything away. Impressive, she thought, for a child that age.

"I'm in kindergarten this year," he said shyly.

"That's wonderful, Billy. Do you have a lot of friends?" Kyla really wanted to help Vivian, but was afraid to offend the woman by offering.

"Not yet, but I just started at my new school," Billy said

and then a sheen of tears appeared in his eyes.

Before Kyla could ask another question, the teapot whistled.

"Do you like cream and sugar with your tea?" Vivian asked.

"Yes to both, please," Kyla answered before thanking Vivian and joining her at the small kitchen table.

"Ah, a woman after my own heart. Not too many people like cream in their tea," she said with a smile.

"I spent a semester of college in London and got used to the overseas habit. Now, I'm hooked," Kyla said with a fond smile. At that moment in her life, everything had been beautiful and the world was at her fingertips. She had never been able to break the European way of drinking her tea, and she hadn't want to.

By the time she left, Kyla had even more questions about Vivian and Billy, and the sadness that seemed to reside in both of their eyes even when they smiled. Hopefully she would get to know them both well enough to feel comfortable asking where his parents were. But what if it was something awful? She didn't know if she could handle that.

Sometimes, questions were better left unanswered. As she moved into her apartment and looked at the picture of her family she kept on her living room wall, she thought of all the unanswered questions she still had about her own life and those nearest and dearest to her.

Curiosity caused pain. Maybe she should just not worry about Vivian and Billy. And yet, as she moved toward her room, she knew that wasn't going to happen. With a sigh, she got ready for bed. This holiday season continued to hang heavy on her shoulders.

CHAPTER EIGHT

THREE DAYS.

It had been three long days and nights, and Tanner hadn't managed to get two seconds alone with his neighbor. Today was the day. He'd been avoiding letting her know that he was Santa, but she was good at avoiding things, too — or rather at avoiding him. He hadn't seen her in the apartment building since the day he moved in.

He'd paced the long, freezing-cold hallways, and he'd already called in to have the heating fixed. They were sure taking their sweet time getting the problem solved, though. How had his tenants put up with this for so long? Anyway, there he paced, hoping Kyla would come out.

She never did.

So here he was at the mall an hour early, with a cup of coffee in his hand. He'd strike up a conversation, ask her out on a date, and they'd go from there.

Oh, hell. What in the world had he been thinking? He couldn't ask her out on a date. He wasn't allowed to go anywhere but the stupid mall and the even stupider apartments. How was he supposed to get laid when he wasn't able to use his best moves?

Wait!

He didn't need to buy her an expensive dinner to get her beneath him. He was great-looking and charming, wasn't he? And he knew how to get a girl. Not that he'd had to do much chasing. Women naturally chased after him. As a matter of fact, he couldn't remember a time he'd had to be the pursuer. Of course, that was when he could flash his money and family name, and he couldn't do that now. This might prove an interesting challenge — courting a dame with just his looks and charm alone. Challenge accepted.

This could be fun.

Stepping into the break room, which also happened to be the changing area, he smiled when he found Kyla sitting on the bench, her costume in hand as she rubbed at her eyes sleepily.

"Good morning," he said.

Her head snapped up and she eyed him warily.

"What are you doing here?" She glanced over at the door as if she thought he was a stalker ready to pounce and she was ensuring a safe exit strategy.

He'd never had *that* reaction before. No, it wasn't quite the ego boost he'd been expecting from her.

"I'm just getting ready to go to work," he said as he

approached — slowly, carefully, unthreateningly, he hoped — and held out the coffee.

She eyed it as if it were poison. Sheesh. His first attempt at giving a woman coffee was an epic fail. Sure, it was mall coffee, but it still had caffeine in it, for crap's sake.

"You work here?"

She still didn't take the offered cup, so Tanner set it down on the bench next to her before heading over to his assigned locker and reaching in for the costume. When he pulled out the Santa suit, her eyes widened.

"You're Santa?" she gasped.

"Yep, been working with you all week," he replied, and he began stripping down to his boxers and tank top before piling the padding on.

"I...uh...didn't know," she said as she stood up stiffly.

Tanner couldn't fail to notice her shooting him what she thought was a covert glance. She didn't look to be too horrified by what she saw, he thought, grinning to himself.

He knew he was a bit arrogant about his looks. Yes, the basics might have been the gift of good genes, but the body was something he worked hard for. He ran regularly, at minimum five days a week, and he lifted weights at the gym as often as his schedule allowed. Well, before he was in a facility without the option. Maybe he should consider having the contractor build a makeshift one just so he had somewhere to burn some of his pent-up time and frustration. Ahh, then again, it was under a month — now about twenty days — until he regained his freedom. His incredible physique could handle it.

"Like what you see?" he asked with his field-tested seductive smile.

She pressed her lips together into a grim slash as she took him in, starting with the bottom of his feet — thick socks covered his ridiculous ankle device, he was happy to remember — and then moving her eyes slowly upward, pausing pointedly on the padding he'd just placed around his middle. Her only reply was an unimpressed raised eyebrow.

"Hey, you're the one who said you had a Santa fetish," he reminded her with a wink.

"I also said that it, whatever *it* is, wasn't going to happen with you," she replied.

"Not exactly. You said I wouldn't get to hear about it. I much prefer show over tell." He could play this game with her all day long if she wanted.

"Let me make myself a bit more clear, then. It won't happen with you. *Ever. Under any circumstances.*"

"That's because you don't know me. I'm a great guy," he said, trying to strike a sexy pose — not too possible in this pathetic fat suit.

"Should I be wowed because I met you for two minutes the other day?"

"Well…yeah," he said, pulling up the large Santa pants after giving up on trying to do anything even remotely resembling sexy.

She laughed. Actually laughed at him. Tanner really

didn't know how to handle that reaction.

"You are quite sure of yourself, Tanner."

Kyla walked into the small bathroom, he assumed to change into her costume. Too bad she wanted to hide. He wouldn't mind seeing her without much on — he'd prefer nothing at all, actually.

When she returned, he gave her an appreciative look, which she ignored. She eyed the coffee as if she really wanted it but was unwilling to take the chance the contents might be poisoned. So he sighed with exasperation, walked over, and picked up the cup. Pulling off the lid while looking straight at her, he took a gulp before putting the lid back on and holding the coffee out to her. "See, it's not poisoned."

"Okay, then," she said. She accepted the cup and took a long swallow, sighing. "Mmm, you obviously pay attention."

Yes, Tanner was very observant. He'd listened as the elves all spoke before they went on coffee runs. He knew she liked extra caramel in her coffee.

"I always pay attention to what a woman wants," he said, using his best come-hither voice. She sauntered toward him with wantonly flared nostrils, parted lips and drooping eyelids, and Tanner was about to spring….um…to his…feet.

When she ran a finger up his padding, Tanner cursed the layers between them. "Good. I like a man who listens," she purred, and leaned closer. He also leaned forward, getting ready to connect their lips.

The flat of her hand slammed against his chest.

He looked at her and waited. Huh?

"Not gonna happen." With that, she turned and sashayed from the room. He was sure the added wiggle in her hips was just for him.

Instead of being angry, he allowed a huge grin to spread across his lips. She was obviously playing hard to get. But if she wanted to be chased, he could certainly accommodate her.

With a whistle springing from his lips, he followed her out the door. He didn't even mind that he was about to be accosted by a pack of stinky kids. His eyes would be glued to her sweet ass the rest of the day anyway.

Well, maybe that wasn't the best idea while he was holding kids on his lap. He'd save the looking for breaks.

CHAPTER NINE

T ANNER'S DAY WAS coming to a close when a small boy climbed up onto him. He had only this last kid to appease and then he could go home. *Let's do this*, he said silently with what little sarcasm he had left after a full day of every sarcastic comment he could think of running through his brain.

"What do you want Santa to bring you for Christmas?" Tanner asked with a half-assed attempt at a Santa chuckle.

The boy peered up with wide eyes and a trembling lip.

Great. Just great.

"Come on, kid. How is Santa going to know what you want if you don't tell him?"

The boy whispered something beneath his breath, but Tanner couldn't hear it, so he leaned down. "What's your name?"

"Billy," the boy whispered.

"Well, Billy, what toys can Santa bring you this year? I'm sure you have a long list."

"I don't want any more toys," he said as a tear slid down his cheek.

Tanner's stomach tightened as he looked at the grief on this child's face. He didn't understand why he cared, but the grief was so obvious. No. It had to just be that the kid was having a bad day. Where in the hell were his parents? He looked out and couldn't see anyone likely.

"Of course you want some toys. Don't all good little boys want toys?"

"I haven't been a good boy," he whispered, a sob coming up from deep down inside.

"How old are you, Billy?" Tanner asked.

"Five."

"Well, don't you want a set of Legos or maybe a Transformer?" Tanner hoped to speed this along.

"No."

"Maybe a racetrack and some cars?"

"I just want my mommy and daddy back," Billy choked out.

Tanner was stopped cold. "What?"

"They went to heaven, my grandma said, but I don't want them to be in heaven. I promised my grandma I would be a good boy, that I wouldn't chase Mary around the playground with my fake snake again. I promised to eat my vegetables. Grandma said it wasn't my fault, but it has to be my fault. I just want them to come back home. I miss my mommy and daddy."

This small child and his devastated eyes left Tanner speechless. How was he supposed to respond to *that*? What could he possibly say to ease the boy's pain?

Nothing.

There was nothing he could say or do. This wasn't something that even his money could fix; it wasn't something tangible that he could put his hands on and twist until it got better. This was grief, and there was nothing but time that would heal it. If even that.

"Billy, it was nothing you did. Sometimes, the people we love the most have to go away. I don't know why, but I bet they are watching out for you every single day, and they're so very proud of you." Tanner just hoped that his flailing around for words didn't screw up this child for the rest of his life.

"Why did they have to leave?" Billy asked, gazing up at Tanner with such innocent eyes.

"I don't know, Billy. Even Santa doesn't have *all* the answers. I do know that they love you very much, though. You are one special little boy."

Billy gave a watery smile, then leaned against Tanner's chest and wrapped his arms around him.

"I love you, Santa," Billy whispered, resting his little head beneath "Santa's" chin, and Tanner's heart felt as if it were going to melt.

What was this small child doing to him?

"I love you, too, Billy." Tanner's voice was slightly

strained. Those were not words he ever spoke, and when he said *never*, he meant *never*. He cleared his throat as he felt an odd sting in his eyes.

Billy held on for several more minutes before he climbed from Tanner's lap and climbed slowly down the steps with the help of one of the elves. He turned back and attempted a smile.

"I know you're magic, Santa, 'cause my mommy always said that Christmas was magic and no dream was impossible when you came. So maybe you can just bring them back," he said, sounding far older than a five-year-old child.

Tanner stood up and moved to Billy, kneeling down in front of him. "All the magic in the world can't undo some things, Billy. I wish it could. Just don't give up on Christmas or the things your mother told you that magic can do," he said with desperation. For some reason it mattered to Tanner that this boy didn't lose his love of Christmas and the magic of Santa.

Billy said no more as he walked away. Tanner watched him, looking for someone to take the young child's hand, but he was still alone as he turned a corner. Who was at the mall with him? Should Tanner go and chase him down? Not knowing what to do, he just kneeled there, emptiness filling him. He'd never experienced a pain like what Billy was currently going through. He'd been too young to feel the impact when his mother had walked out on him and his siblings, and his family was close — or they had been close until the last few years.

But even that was changing again and he was speaking to his siblings a little more — really speaking to them — and even to his father. To top that off, he'd discovered he had all of these cousins. He'd never been alone and afraid like the child who'd just looked so trustingly into his eyes.

If Tanner was alone, it was by choice.

When he looked up, Tanner's eyes connected with Kyla's and she didn't even try to hide the tears streaming down her face. She came toward him and touched his shoulder.

"You did a very good thing there," she whispered before turning and walking away.

Tanner was stunned. After several long moments, he rose to his feet and went through the mall to the changing area. He needed to get as far from this place as he possibly could.

This Christmas couldn't come and go fast enough.

CHAPTER TEN

UNABLE TO SHAKE the image of the boy with so much pain etched in his features, Tanner decided to trudge back to the apartment building instead of taking a cab. He tried to blank his mind during the fifteen-minute walk, but the boy's face refused to leave his vision. What he needed, obviously, was a good night of sleep. Halloween was long gone, and he refused to be haunted.

As he pulled open the ridiculously heavy front door, he found himself looking at the building through new eyes. A couple of kids were playing in the hallway, laughing as they chased marbles on the ragged floors.

Just yesterday, he'd growled the words *noise pollution* to himself as he passed other children in the building. Now the laughter almost cheered him. Almost, but not quite. These people considered this their home, their place of safety, but he'd done everything in his power to take them away from it.

He never looked at individuals, just the whole of a situation.

Was it profitable? What could it do for him?

But, hey, he was a businessman, trying to make a lot of money for a lot of individuals. That didn't make him a monster. He was just living the American dream. Wasn't that what everyone wanted?

So he wasn't the bad guy here. Businesses weren't charities, and it would be insane to start thinking that way. But this punishment was taking its toll on him. He had to get out of here before he had a meltdown, or became empathetic. He didn't know which would be worse.

Coming around the corner, he heard raised voices and went on instant alert. What in the hell was going on now? This place was just a barrel of fun each time he stepped into it. One minute he saw children playing, the next someone shouting. What would be next? Dancing monkeys?

Instead, he saw two men pinning Kyla between them, her face panicked, and fury rose within him.

"Stop!" she cried just before one of the men leaned in and mashed his lips against hers.

The man right in front of her leaned back only slightly to ogle her again. "Come on, baby. I saw the way you were looking at me in the mall."

He held her arms pinned behind her back and ground his hips against her. His accomplice laughed, and both of her assailants had their hands all over her.

"Please stop," she cried.

"Not until we're finished. Get her key, Mike."

Why hadn't anyone come out to help?

Tanner moved swiftly forward, and before the accomplice knew what was happening, Tanner grabbed his shoulder, spun him around, and slammed his fist against his eye. One down; one to go.

The main attacker instantly released Kyla, then reached into his pocket and pulled out a knife. "Ah, ya think you're gonna be a hero today, do ya?" the man taunted.

Tanner said nothing, but he looked unflinchingly at the weapon the man was swinging around. Kyla had backed away and was also watching the flashing blade.

"I got no problem spilling your blood," the man said, and he lunged forward.

Tanner stepped to the left, then kicked the man's knees, making him scream in pain, drop to the ground and lose his grip on his knife, all in a moment's time. One more swift kick to the guy's head and the asshole was moaning on the hallway floor.

Tanner kept his eyes firmly on both of the men. "Call the police," he told Kyla brusquely.

With trembling fingers, she pulled out her key and wrenched her apartment door open, then rushed inside to grab her phone. Tanner waited for the police to arrive.

Kyla didn't reappear immediately, probably terrified that they'd try to attack again. The officers showed up soon and hauled the men out to their police car, then came back in and knocked on Kyla's door, to interview her about the assault. When Tanner saw her again, he noticed the bruise forming on her cheek. For the second time that day, his stomach clenched.

How could any man hit a woman? He might not have treated all his dates with the utmost respect, but he'd certainly never abused them. The women he dated knew the score, knew he would wine and dine them. He didn't *expect* sex, but if that's how the evening ended — and it always did — it was mutually pleasurable.

He was repelled by the thought of what those men had done and had been trying to do. Freaking animals. No. No. Those humans were far worse than most animals. It sickened him.

"Come on," he told Kyla when they found themselves standing alone in the hallway, the dirtbags gone in the back of a police cruiser.

She looked at him warily when he held out his hand. He didn't want to scare her further, so he gave her his most trustworthy smile and waited. Finally, she wrapped her fingers in his and let him lead her into his apartment. After sitting her down at his dining table, he got a washcloth and put some ice in it.

Kneeling in front of her, he paused as he brought his hand up and ran his fingers softly across her swelling cheek. "I'm so sorry this happened, Kyla."

Damn security!

It wasn't something he'd even thought the building needed, which was foolish on his part. There were single women and children here in a less than respectable area of Seattle. A front lobby area was available. It wouldn't be that difficult to have twenty-four-hour security present and keypads on all outside doors.

"They followed me home from the mall. I don't understand guys like that," she said, obviously upset, but holding herself together extremely well under the circumstances.

"They aren't real men," he said, raising the washcloth and placing it gently against her cheek.

"No, they aren't," she agreed, and her lips turned up just the tiniest bit.

"I'm sorry I didn't get here sooner. I'm sorry they had the opportunity to hit you." *I'm sorry I was too cheap to add security to the building,* he added silently.

"I'm just glad you showed up when you did, that it wasn't worse than it was. I've never had a problem here before — not to that extent. The worst that's happened in two years is the occasional drunken neighbor trying to talk me into a date. I just…" She stopped when tears filled her eyes and she started to choke up.

He was amazed she was able to sit there so calmly. "How did you end up here?" Okay, not so calmly; she flinched at that question. But Tanner went on. "From what I've observed over the last few days, you seem smart, too smart to be working as an elf and living in a dump like this."

"It doesn't matter," she said, squirming in the chair in front of him.

"I want to know."

"I…life happens."

"Yes. Sometimes situations are beyond our control, Kyla. But I have a feeling there's a lot more to you than meets the eye."

"I don't want to talk about it," she said, and her eyes met his with a challenging gleam.

He respected her bravery. "Sometimes it can help to speak to a stranger." He didn't know why he was pushing her, why it mattered. He should just give her the ice pack, lead her back to her apartment, and walk away. This woman was obviously too complicated, not his usual type at all.

He was stuck in this place, though, stuck here for another twenty-one days. And he found himself wanting to know her story, wanting to connect with her. It was probably just because he was bored, he told himself, that she'd piqued his curiosity, but there seemed to be something else there, something he couldn't identify. *Stupid.*

"You can talk to me. I won't repeat what you say. You never know…it might help," he said, pushing back some loose strands of her hair as he watched the indecision flash in her eyes. He was surprised when she began speaking in an unutterably quite voice.

"A couple of years ago, I was with my family on vacation and there was a wreck. I lived. They didn't," she said with a shrug, as if she were over it, as if it were no big deal. But the pain radiating from every pore of her body contradicted the way she forced out those words with such feigned casualness.

"I can't imagine," Tanner said, completely out of his element, not knowing what he should say for the second time that day. Twice now, someone was telling him about losing parents way too soon. Was this fate that they had met? No! He didn't believe in fate or any other hogwash like that. It was merely a coincidence. That was all.

But, fool that he was, he went on. "Did you have siblings?" He knew he should have shut up, let this go, but he couldn't seem to control his mouth. And he had been the one to push her to speak.

Her eyes flashed with pain even more raw than before. "A little brother," she said in a whisper.

"Oh, Kyla, that has to be really tough." How lame, but that was all he could say.

"Those are the standard words I hear. It's okay, Tanner. It happened almost two years ago. Almost to the day."

"Christmas?" he asked, horrified.

"Two days before."

Damn. He really had no clue what to say to her, no clue at all.

She looked down at the floor as she tried to compose herself. "I need to get back to my place," she said softly. She brought her hand up and pushed at his fingers, which were still holding the ice to her cheek.

Tanner pulled them away, wincing at the sight of her delicate cheekbone; a slight bruise marred her features, but only that. At least the swelling had already gone down. He was glad he'd arrived when he did — it could have been so much worse. He set the washcloth aside and slid his thumb tenderly across the cruel mark before resting his hand against her neck.

Her gaze locked with his and she shivered. Almost against his will, Tanner found himself leaning forward, coming closer to her as his other hand rose and his fingers wrapped around the soft strands of her hair.

When Kyla didn't pull back, Tanner closed the gap between them and kissed her, just a slight brushing of his lips against hers. When her sweet breath fanned out across his mouth in a shocked gasp, he deepened the kiss, tasting her lips with his and tightening his fingers on her scalp.

Kyla's lips moved beneath his and her hands came up to grip his shoulders. When her breasts brushed against his chest, blood raced through his body and rushed instantly to one very sensitive location. The simple sigh that escaped her throat wasn't helping; hell, it was far more erotic than the full-on striptease his last partner had treated him to.

He pulled back and looked into her eyes. "Kyla," he whispered. He wanted her in his bed — right now.

She smiled, her eyes glazed, and she ran her tongue along her bottom lip, delighting in his taste, making his groin tighten even more painfully. Then, as he leaned forward, the spell was somehow broken. Her eyes flew open and the hands that had been resting against his shoulders stiffened; she pushed him away.

He wanted to lean back against her, take her into his arms, and show her how good it was going to be between the two of them. But that would make him no better than the monsters who'd just tried to force themselves on her.

"I have to go," she said, a fit of trembling racking her body.

"I'll walk you home."

He stood up, and then, much to his surprise, she smiled.

"I live just a few steps from your door, Tanner."

"I'm a gentleman. I always walk my dates home and make sure they get inside safely."

"This was a date?" she scoffed, clearly trying to downplay the intense moment they'd just shared.

"I got a kiss from you. I'd say it was a pretty great date."

"Well, then, you are a cheapskate date. I didn't even get a meal."

Tanner was shocked by her words. She was able to joke like this so soon after being attacked by two loathsome stalkers? One minute, she seemed so vulnerable, and then the next, confident and in control. Was it all an act to protect herself? Or to maybe drive him insane?

"I'll feed you right now, sweetheart. Then I'll feed you again…in the morning," he added with a wicked smile.

"I'll pass. I already got the goodnight kiss," she said, and she moved toward his door.

Tanner followed her into the hall and waited as she pushed her door open with a swift thump of her hip to unstick it, and then she moved inside.

She turned around and looked at him for a moment, making his heart leap. Was she going to invite him in? He took a step forward.

"'Night, Tanner," she said, closing her door a little before looking at him again. "Thank you." Pain replaced the amusement in her eyes. She shook her head as if clearing it, and then she disappeared into her apartment.

Tanner stood there for several moments, just staring at her door. He should simply call this one a loss — she was far too complicated for what he was looking for. He just wanted a woman to satisfy his needs, primal and nothing more, while he was stuck under house arrest in this place of doom and gloom. There was no way he wanted a relationship, for Christ's sake

But when he closed the door to his apartment and walked over to the chair she'd been sitting in, he knew he wasn't going to stop pursuing her. She intrigued him too much. Besides, he now looked at her as a challenge, and he'd *never* been able to resist a challenge.

He just had to figure out what his next move was going to be.

After cleaning up, Tanner ordered takeout, then grabbed his laptop, grateful for the mobile Internet connection he'd managed to get. It was slow, but at least it was something. For some reason, though, he couldn't force himself to work. There was a first for everything, he supposed.

Several hours later he found himself lying in bed wide awake, thinking of one blue-eyed woman who was stirring him in ways he didn't want to be stirred, and he was even contemplating what life would be like in her shoes.

No matter how much he tried convincing himself that this was about the conquest, he couldn't quite put Kyla into the neat little box he'd set up for her.

Damn!

CHAPTER ELEVEN

KYLA KEPT PACING back and forth, unsure in which direction she should go. She walked toward Tanner's door, and then retreated to her own, her hands outstretched as she held the warm plate of cookies.

Saturday morning. She was assuming he'd be home now, since he'd worked Monday through Friday at the mall. She had her other job to go to in a few hours, but for now she was home and she really wanted to say thank you to the man who'd helped her the night before last. What he'd done had been kind — more than that, of course — and she needed to do something. Approaching his door again, she lifted her hand…then it dropped, and she groaned in disgust with herself.

"Oh my gosh, just knock on his fricking door," she mumbled in exasperation as she reached up again.

Instead of knocking, she walked away and then wanted to

kick herself for being such a coward. He'd helped her, saved her from who knows what was going to happen, and then soothed her before, like a gentleman, really, before giving her a heart-stopping kiss. She owed him at least a warm batch of homemade cookies. But no matter how much she told herself to knock on his door, she couldn't muster the courage.

"It's not like you have a crush on him." Sheesh. What was it with this talking to herself? Were the doctors going to come in and drag her off to the loony bin?

"Can I help you, ma'am?"

The deep male voice stopped Kyla in her tracks. It was daytime, and she'd never had a problem in this apartment complex until those men attacked her, so she didn't know why the shiver of fear ran down her spine. Shaking it off, Kyla turned and saw a man in a blue uniform with a silver badge on his breast pocket. He was staring at her.

"Who are you?" She knew that the way she said it was slightly rude, but she was surprised as sin to see a man who looked so official standing there in the building.

"I'm with the new security company the owner of the building hired. We've been watching you on camera pacing the hallway for the last fifteen minutes, so I just want to find out if there's anything I can help you with."

"There are security cameras?" Dumbfounded, she looked up at the low ceilings, trying to spot them.

"They're being installed throughout the building, but this floor has been completed. We're setting up our station in the front lobby. You should find a notice in your mailbox about the update."

Kyla hadn't been aware that any of this activity was going on. Of course, she hadn't left her apartment the day before — not even once — but still, she should have noticed something, or maybe clued in to the noise that must have been happening in her hallway. No wonder she'd been a victim the other night. She just wasn't all that observant.

"I...uh...no...I don't need help," she finally said, remembering he'd asked.

"Are you sure, ma'am? You've been pacing for quite a while," he said as he looked behind her.

"No," she said with a sigh, before handing him the plate of warm cookies. "One of the tenants did something really nice for me the other night and I wanted to bring him cookies, but now I realize that was a really stupid idea, and so I've been trying to knock on his door, but I just can't do it, so you take the dang cookies and give them to the other guards. It's my welcome. I'm so glad you're here." What a lot of rambling! She must sound like an utter loon!

He held the cookies away from him as if there might be bugs in them or something, and he eyed her warily.

"I can't accept gifts," he said, no smile in either his face or his tone.

"It's not like it's a bribe or something. They're just warm cookies," she said, instantly irritated with him. She'd spent all morning baking. The least someone — anyone — could do was take the stupid things and eat them. Okay, okay, and tell her they were wonderful, of course.

"I really appreciate it, ma'am, but I can't accept your cookies," he said, trying again to hand them back.

"You're being rude," she said, stamping her foot. But this was ridiculous. Why in the world was she fighting about cookies?

"Ma'am—"

He was interrupted.

"Just say *thank you*, Steve, and take the cookies." Another guard had walked up, a man little shorter than the first one, but with a much more friendly demeanor.

"You know we can't accept cookies, Wayne," Steve snapped.

"Ma'am, are your cookies poisoned?" Wayne asked.

Kyla looked at him for a moment without knowing what to say. She'd given away a lot of cookies in her life and had never once been asked that question.

"No," she finally murmured and looked back and forth between the two men.

"Good enough for me," Wayne said before pulling the plastic wrap off the plate Steve was still holding and grabbing a cookie. "Delicious."

Kyla beamed at the man and refused to look at the first guard again. How hard had it been to accept a gift? Granted, the cookies had been intended for Tanner, but she was just glad someone had taken them.

"I'm going back to the front," Steve said, thrusting the plate at Wayne before spinning on his heel and heading the opposite direction.

"I'm sorry about Steve. He's a 'by the books all the way' kind of guy. My philosophy is to just live a little." Wayne finished his cookie and grabbed another one.

"I like that philosophy so much better. Life is short. Why not enjoy it?" She knew she was grinning goofily, but she'd just been through several tense moments and now she felt like laughing. It was silly. Maybe she needed a spa day — not that she could afford that.

"What's your name?"

"Kyla Ridgley," she answered, extending her hand.

"Wayne Stint," he replied, accepting her hand and squeezing.

"It was great to meet you, Wayne. I'm going to go back to my baking now," she said before realizing he was still holding on to her hand.

He reached the same realization at the same time, and his cheeks flushed. He let go quickly and mumbled "Sorry."

"No problem." She stood there awkwardly a moment longer before she decided to just turn and walk away.

Making it back to her apartment, Kyla leaned against the door and sighed before she called herself all sorts of names. She should have just taken the cookies to Tanner. She still could. She had a lot more to make.

But she knew she wasn't going to do it.

CHAPTER TWELVE

WELL, LOOK AT what we have here!"
Tanner froze. He didn't need to turn around
to recognize that voice. Dammit! Dammit!
Dammit! His life was really going to hell.

"Mmm, what a very sexy Santa Claus you make. I heard
the good news, but I had to come see it for myself."

Jokes and guffaws at Tanner's expense flew thick and fast.
With a thunderous expression on his face — sadly obscured
by his white beard and bushy eyebrows — he glared at his
brother Crew and cousin Lucas.

"Do you guys have a reason for being here?" he snapped
as he looked around to see whether any of his other relatives
were nearby. He'd really hoped that the visit at his apartment
a little over a week ago would be the only such surprise.

"Nope. Just had to come and see how charming you look
in your Santa costume," Crew said.

"What a peach you are, big brother," Tanner growled, and he began walking away.

"Now, now, don't be in such a hurry. We thought we'd take you out for a beer. I'm sure you could use it," Lucas said, easily keeping up.

"Very funny, Lucas. You both know I'm under flipping house arrest. The only place I get to go now is to my wonderfully quaint apartment — that is, if I don't get mugged on the way there," he said as he reached the break room and began yanking the Santa suit off.

"Well, then, I guess we'll just have to drink a couple of beers in your new digs," Crew said. "I'm looking forward to checking the place out."

"What if I'd rather not have the company?" Tanner didn't want to take a chance that he'd run into Kyla while these guys were around. If she came up and spoke to him, they'd get ideas. He didn't want them getting ideas. As soon as he was done with this sentence, he was out of here and he wouldn't look back. He shouldn't need to worry about it, though, as he hadn't seen her since last Thursday, when she'd been attacked. That was four days ago, and he wasn't happy about it.

"You have to be bored out of your mind," Lucas said. "Of course you want the company."

"I'm not going to get you two to go away, am I?"

"Not a chance," Crew said, sitting down and relaxing, even though the bench was absurdly uncomfortable.

"Fine. Give me a few minutes to change and you can give

me a ride back. I get sick of taking stinking cabs or the bus. The walk takes too damn long after being at this mall all day. Kyla likes the walk, though — says it relaxes her."

Tanner wanted to bite his tongue off as soon as the words popped from his mouth. There was no hope the two of them hadn't noticed his slip.

"Kyla?" they said in unison, eyebrows raised.

"Don't," Tanner replied, and added a glare to let them know it was a closed subject.

"Hmm, have you managed to find romance in the projects?" Crew asked.

"The apartments aren't the projects, and no, I haven't. Even if I had, I certainly wouldn't tell *you* about it."

"I think you're protesting a little too much, cuz," Lucas said with a big grin.

Tanner had met his Anderson cousins a year ago or just a little more. He hadn't known of their existence until then, thanks to a very desperate doctor who'd kidnapped his father when he was a newborn. But it was as if they'd all been together their entire lives. All of them got along beautifully, and none of them had a problem with flinging crap at each other.

"How could I have met someone? I'm under house arrest," Tanner reminded them, trying his best to sound convincing.

"You do have a point there, but you *are* staying in an apartment building, not an all-male prison facility," Crew told his brother. "I think meeting someone is a definite possibility."

"Fine. I did meet a woman, but it's not what you think. She's an elf." Again, if he could kick his own ass, he would.

"An elf? Oh, this just keeps getting better and better," Lucas said with a Santa-like belly laugh.

"I think there's an adult movie or two with Santa and his elves," Crew managed to choke out in the midst of an explosion of his own guffaws.

"You're both dumbasses," Tanner said as he buttoned his coat, and left the room. There was no way he was continuing that conversation. But he knew the two of them were right on his heels, because their laughter followed him out of the mall.

"Where are you parked?" Tanner practically growled.

"This way," Lucas said, trying his hardest to suppress his merriment now.

Tanner was really hoping they were driving a truck. Then he could sit in the bed and ignore both of them. Or maybe he could just jump from the vehicle as it was going down the road and land himself in the hospital for the rest of his sentence. Either option sounded all right with him.

When they reached the car — not a trunk, dammit — Tanner climbed in back, and, miracle of miracles, his two tormentors kept silent for the short ride back to the apartment building.

When they made it inside without running into Kyla, Tanner breathed a huge sigh of relief. If the two of them saw how unbelievably gorgeous his elfin neighbor really was, they'd be right back to harassing him, and they'd keep at it for the rest of the night.

Instead, they popped open a few beers that they'd had in a cooler, and they sat down, the joking over with as the three of them talked about the pros and cons of remodeling versus starting fresh. By the end of the conversation, Tanner was torn. He couldn't alter his plans. That would be foolish.

However...

He wanted new, but he knew he might not get his way — damned judge! — so he needed to have a plan B. No! He wouldn't change his mind.

If only the what-if thoughts about Kyla didn't keep running through his head.

"Some of us aren't locked into this apartment building, so we're going to get out of here now," Lucas said with a sly look at Tanner.

"Yeah. Yeah. Enjoy your fun, but one of these days you're going to find your ass in a similar situation."

"I don't think so, cousin," Lucas said as a knock sounded on the door. "I'll get it."

Lucas swung the door open, and before Tanner could stop him, he felt his cheeks instantly heat up. Kyla was standing there in the opening with a shy smile, but her cheeks reddened, too, when she noticed Lucas and then looked past him to where Tanner was standing awkwardly next to his brother.

"My, my, my, a hot girl delivering cookies," Lucas said as he turned to wink at Tanner. "Maybe I shouldn't be in such a hurry to leave."

"Shut up, Lucas." Tanner was finally able to make his feet work and he moved to the door, pushing Lucas out of the way. "Hi, Kyla. What's going on?"

The smell of her freshly baked cookies was wafting from her open apartment door and Tanner's mouth watered. As much as he didn't want his brother or cousin to meet Kyla, the deed was done, and he found himself wanting to drag her into the room and devour her, take her temptingly pouty mouth with his own and kiss it, kiss it, kiss it ...

"I...uh...baked some cookies as a thank-you," she murmured.

Tanner could barely hear her.

"Cookies? I love cookies," Crew said as he walked up next to Tanner.

Kyla could do nothing more than gape at Tanner's brother in surprise as he reached out and took the plate.

And her surprise didn't end there.

"Thanks, Kyla. I'll talk to you later." Tanner did the rudest thing he'd ever done in his life and shut the door in her face. Yes, his brother and cousin had seen her, but if she now disappeared, the ribbing should be minimal. He absolutely didn't want his family to torment him with questions about her, even though he knew at least a few were coming his way. The damage had been done.

"Hot damn! She's a beauty, *and* she bakes. I'd keep her," Crew said as he bit into a still-warm cookie.

"Hands off," Tanner told him. "Those are for me." He snatched up the plate and walked away. If he didn't respond to the taunting, maybe they'd just let it drop.

Fat chance.

"*She's* for you? Or her *cookies* are?" Lucas was obviously amused by himself and his so-called wit.

Not funny. Yeah. Tanner knew they couldn't possibly let this one go. He wouldn't have let it go if the situation was reversed, but that was beside the point. This was him on the receiving end, and he didn't like it, didn't like it one little bit.

"Weren't you guys just leaving?" he said, praying that Kyla wasn't on the other side of the door as he yanked it back open. Thankfully, she was gone.

"I don't want to leave now," Crew said. "Things just got interesting."

"Tough. I'm going to bed," Tanner told them.

"At nine?" Lucas asked. "You're becoming an old man."

"Yeah, yeah. Well, you've been here a couple hours and you've already overstayed your welcome. Now, get out of here before I tell your wives what great guys the two of you are."

There was a short pause. After they threw a few more lame jokes Tanner's way, they finally exited his apartment. Tanner shut the door then leaned against it in frustration. If only Kyla had waited ten more minutes to show up… This night could have ended a hell of a lot better.

CHAPTER THIRTEEN

TANNER SLAMMED THE door to his apartment. Another day at the mall — it felt like he'd been there a year — and he was sticky, irritated, and in desperate need of a hot shower.

He hadn't managed to see Kyla the last couple days, since she hadn't been at the mall performing her North Pole duties. Of course that thought led to another, that there was another pole he'd love to show her, one that was definitely pointing north. Yeah, he was a pig. He shook his head, disgusted with himself.

Anyway, knocking on her door had done him no good. He was beginning to think that she'd possibly up and moved from the building. Sure, he'd slammed the door in her face, but that was a minor offense wasn't it? Okay, he'd yet to meet a woman who was forgiving after getting such a cold shoulder, but she should at least give him a chance to apologize.

But he couldn't fault her if she had moved to better pastures. The place was a dump. As soon as his punishment was over, he wasn't setting foot in these doors again — not until he managed to get a demolition crew in and he could personally direct the first wrecking ball through its thick walls. Starting, of course, with the very apartment he was imprisoned in.

After taking as long a shower as the ridiculously small hot-water tank would allow, Tanner stepped from the tub and was grateful no one was around to see all his goose bumps from the freezing-cold room. He was wrapping a towel around his waist when he heard a knock on his door.

He wasn't expecting anyone.

He moved toward the door, and then realized his ankle monitor was on full display, so he rushed back to his room and threw on thick socks. But he didn't have the time or the energy to do anything about the towel, which was the only other thing covering him. If his visitor had a problem with it, he or she shouldn't knock on his door.

Beyond irritated and shivering, he stomped over and flung the door open, and then just stood there at a loss for words. Standing before him was a large green pine tree, real needles and all. The smell of the freshly cut tree filled the air and brought back happy childhood memories — ones he quickly tried to squash back down.

"I didn't know trees knew how to knock," he said, and much to his surprise, he laughed. Was he bipolar? He couldn't quite rule that out. After all, he was ready to growl one minute, and the next he was laughing. At the very least he was getting permanent brain damage from who knew what that was seeping from the building's walls.

Kyla's head popped around the tree and then Tanner's ego swelled at the way her eyes widened as they traveled over his half-naked body.

Hmm, maybe he would get his sexy neighbor into his bed after all.

* * * * *

Kyla hated to admit it, but one look at the guy had knocked the breath from her lungs. Tanner was a fine specimen when he had clothes on — okay, in anything but that Santa suit. In a tank top and boxers, he was breathtaking. Magnificent. Wrapped in nothing but a towel, with droplets of water sliding down those solid pecs, he was too good to be true. Talk about a ripped torso.

When she realized she was standing there practically drooling, she snapped her gaze back to his knowing – hell, almost gloating — eyes and tried to form a coherent sentence.

"I...uh...thought you might like to have a Christmas tree for your new place," she mumbled.

Her impulsive act had probably been pretty foolish, especially since he'd slammed the door in her face the last time she'd seen him. She couldn't explain why she was doing this. It was just that the man *had* helped her the other day, and he seemed lonely, didn't he? Maybe he'd shut the door on her because the men in his apartment had been bill collectors or he had a gambling problem and they were there to collect.

Okay. Fine. Even if she was curious, and she was, she wasn't going to ask. But if he slammed the door in her face again, she would take the hint and stay away, like she should be doing right now. She was just trying to spread the Christmas spirit, something she hadn't wanted to do in two years, not since she'd lost her family. Since it was the first time she'd even thought of having a tree after that horrible "holiday" two years before, she'd bought one — and brought it to him. It was just too painful still to have the tree in her own apartment.

Now she was regretting her impulsive act. Tanner was too worldly and cynical to go for such a holiday tradition.

"It's good to see you, Kyla. And I like the tree. Please come in." Did he sound a bit stiff? Probably. He took the tree from her and dragged it inside the apartment. "You haven't been at the mall. Did you quit?"

One of the branches snagged the bottom of his towel; she held her breath and waited, eyes peeled. Sadly, the towel stayed in place. When he leaned the tree against the wall and turned back to her, she jerked her gaze up and met his eyes again, realizing he'd asked a question that she'd never answered.

"I…um…have another job, so I only work part time at

the mall," she said before taking a long breath and trying to sound a little less ditzy. "I don't need to stay. I just wanted to drop this off and…I'll…uh…be going now." Kyla stumbled as she backed toward his door.

"You can't just drop off the tree and run. I'll need help decorating it," he said. His large frame filled the doorway, blocking her exit. "Also, I need to apologize for…um… shutting the door in your face the other day. It was just that the guys that were here were…" He trailed off awkwardly and his cheeks flushed.

She knew it. Those two guys were thugs. That had to be it!

"No need to explain. I wasn't offended," she lied. "And you can decorate the tree however you like. It was just a spur-of-the-moment thing. You did me a great favor a few days ago, and I wanted to find a way to show my appreciation beyond the…um…cookies."

"I do appreciate the tree, Kyla, and the cookies," he said, but his expression — it was almost a leer — had her stomach dropping. "Both things are really sweet. Now let me repay the kindness. I ordered pizza right before I jumped into the shower, so join me and we'll throw on a few decorations."

She found that she actually *wanted* to help him. She *really* wanted to keep looking at his indecently clad body.

"Well, I guess I *could* help," she muttered as her eyes drifted to his chest again. It should be illegal to have a body that chiseled. If all of Seattle could see him, the man would prove lethal to half the people there — maybe a bit more than half.

"Thanks," he said, then walked over to his fridge and pulled out a bottle of wine. She didn't know her wine, but it didn't look like a cheap grocery store brand.

"Don't you think you should get dressed first?" she croaked out as she stepped up to the counter. She would never be able to stay here in his apartment with him looking like this. Not without succumbing to every temptation known to man or woman, anyway.

"I just got out of the shower. Sorry," he said blithely, and he took a sip of his wine. He didn't appear to be the least bit apologetic.

"I shouldn't have just barged in. I'll go ahead and wait while you dress." *Please, go dress*, she thought.

With a shockingly smug smile, Tanner passed by her, far too close for comfort. The fragrance of his body wash hit her point-blank, making her inhale extra deeply. She *really* wanted to run her fingers down his perfect chest — just once, she thought. But she somehow managed to keep her hands to herself, though her eyes devoured him as he disappeared into his bedroom.

He left that door open, damn him, and it took all her willpower not to stretch her neck. The thought that he'd be standing in there completely naked for a few moments was making her pant like a… She stopped that thought and turned away from the door to face his empty kitchen counters.

"I don't have any ornaments, so what are we going to use?"

Kyla jumped when Tanner spoke right into her ear from only a couple of inches away. She'd have been quite the happy girl if he'd decided to just slip his hands around her and pull her back against his chest.

Spinning, she angled around him, cursing her traitorous body. No, she wouldn't allow this stranger to make her lose her mind.

It might be too late, her body taunted.

"We'll do popcorn strands," she said desperately.

Tanner gave her with a blank look. "Popcorn?"

"Haven't you ever made popcorn strands?" she asked, and he shook his head. "Gee, Tanner. Not even in elementary school?"

"Nope," he replied, refilling her glass.

Kyla was shocked. She'd somehow drained the first glass of wine in no time flat.

"Well, then, you're in for an experience. I'll be right back. I have some things we'll need in my apartment."

She rushed from his place back to hers and gathered up all the supplies not only for popcorn strands but for some other homemade ornaments as well. Cheap decorating was simple if you had an ounce of knowledge and a desire to do arts and crafts. As she took a minute to control her breathing, she looked at the things she'd amassed with a bit of sadness.

Making popcorn strands for the trees outside had been a tradition in her family. Her dad loved feeding the birds and squirrels, and they'd all had so much fun threading mountains of popcorn and berries. Of course, her family had eaten as much in goodies as they'd put on the strings, and always did so to the sounds of the Rat Pack singing Christmas songs.

Kyla didn't know what had possessed her to buy those things this morning. One minute she'd been doing a little grocery shopping, and the next she'd been checking out with popcorn and cranberries in her cart. That was before she'd even ended up at the Christmas tree lot. There weren't even any trees outside the apartment building. The act had been completely senseless. Well, it had been until now.

Maybe her mom had been there with her, and *she'd* put the items in the cart. The thought made Kyla's eyes sting — but she was finished feeling sad and refused to shed more tears. It was time to embrace some happiness.

When she came back into Tanner's apartment, she found him nailing a couple of boards onto the bottom of the tree, and she watched as the muscles in his shoulders flexed with the swinging of the hammer before he stood and propped the tree up on its makeshift stand.

"I didn't take you for the kind of man who could handle a hammer and nails," she told him. She set down the tree stand she'd grabbed — too late! — and then placed her packages on the kitchen counter. Next, she found a frying pan, put it on the heat, and poured in two tablespoons of oil to it with one kernel. When the kernel popped, she added half a cup of popcorn and waited for the party in the pan to happen. "Hey, Tanner, can you grab a big bowl?"

He went over to the cupboard and took down the bowl. "I prefer not to be categorized. There are a lot of things I can do that would shock you." His wink had her blood stirring.

"I'll just bet there are," she said. She certainly couldn't compete with his level of flirting, but she wasn't going to just stand there in shock all night, either.

"I'd be glad to show you," he offered. And once again, he was suddenly far too close.

"Why don't I take the lead and show you how to make popcorn strands?" She gave a nervous laugh and pushed him back, her hand nearly sizzling when it made contact with his rock-hard chest.

"I have much better ideas on what would be fun," he said, boxing her in against the counter.

Tempted.

But her reasonable side kicked in before she could do something rash, and she brushed past him. Tearing open the bag of cranberries, she put them in a bowl, then grabbed the bag with string and large sewing needles in it.

"Make yourself useful and thread a couple of needles," she said before moving back to the counter and picking up her glass of wine. It really was good, and right now, she needed it.

The sound of the corn popping served as a distraction, and once the large bowl was filled with the puffed kernels, the two of them moved into his living room and began making decorations from opposite sides of his couch.

"Why is your stay in these apartments temporary?" she

asked as she began slipping popcorn onto her string. "Isn't that what you said?"

He watched for a moment and then began imitating her, alternating between popcorn and cranberries.

"It's a long, boring story," he finally answered.

"I don't mind listening. I have a few long, boring stories of my own if you want to hear," she said with a brittle laugh. She didn't really mean that. It wasn't as if this man would want to hear anything about her. In reality she *was* pretty boring, or so she thought.

"Let's just say I was…dared," he told her, forcing a smile.

"You were dared to live here?"

"Sort of," he said with a sigh. "My family is…complicated. I have three brothers and a sister, and we all kind of…well… went our separate ways. So my dad stepped in and decided we needed projects to do." Tanner stopped cold, unwilling to elaborate.

"I'm thoroughly confused right now. What does your living here and your father giving you projects have to do with anything?"

"Hey. Don't stop working on the Christmas tree ornaments," he told her, and she began stringing her goodies again. "I don't know how to explain it other than to say that he decided we were all a little spoiled and wanted to see us doing something different with our lives."

"Are you spoiled?"

Tanner laughed as his eyes met hers, and Kyla couldn't figure out how to get the dang popcorn on her string. She felt like he was holding her prisoner with his gaze, and the reality was that she didn't want to be freed.

His expression changed. He set down his own length of string, scooted closer to her, and, gently removing the string she was working on from her fingers, he raised a hand and cupping her cheek.

"You make me feel, Kyla," he whispered, and then he leaned in and caressed her lips with his.

She forgot all about her question to him, or the fact that he hadn't answered it.

Kyla couldn't breathe as his hand moved back and he let his fingers drift through her hair. She knew she should stop this, but she didn't know why. When he tugged her closer and lifted her onto his lap, she didn't hesitate to wrap her arms around his neck and lean in against his solid body. "You make me forget," she murmured.

And he did. He made her forget it all.

"I want you to forget about anything other than me," he said before closing what little gap was left between them and kissing her with so much heat, she was sure she'd see scorch marks on his couch.

When his hands traveled beneath the hem of her shirt and up the naked skin of her back, she knew she had to decide what she was going to do next. It was too soon for this, and he was a stranger. She wasn't ready to make love to him.

Pulling back, she looked into his eyes and nearly changed her mind. So much fire burned in his gaze. That heat was for her, and only her, at least at this moment.

"I think we should finish the decorations," she said lamely. Was he going to just end up disgusted with her and ask her to leave? That wouldn't shock her.

His hand was still up the back of her shirt and he paused in the act of caressing her skin. His eyes still burned into hers. "Are you sure that's what you want?" he asked, leaning forward and nipping her bottom lip, making heat travel straight to her core.

"No," she admitted. "But it's what I need to do."

"Okay, then." With that, he bent forward and gave her one more small, chaste kiss, and then he slid to the other end of the couch and picked his string back up. When she sat there speechless and dazed, he looked up. "If you continue looking at me like that, I will listen to your eyes and not your mouth," he warned her.

Her eyes widened and for just the briefest of moments she wished he would take control away from her. But she knew she couldn't think like that. With shaky hands she picked up her yarn and began stringing popcorn and cranberries again. It was a mindless task, and she needed that now.

Everything felt awkward for only a few more minutes and then Kyla found herself laughing as Tanner joked with her, often getting up and brushing against her, but not reaching in for a kiss again.

Once the popcorn and the cranberry strands were done, she brought out some white paper and taught him how to make snowflakes. The pizza arrived, and their time together couldn't have been better as her stomach filled with pizza, Christmas goodies, and wine.

When they looked at their finished project, she was overflowing with pride. It was a childish tree filled with strings of popcorn, cranberries, and paper snowflakes, and it was also the most wonderful thing she'd seen in a long, long while.

"Thank you, Kyla. I haven't enjoyed decorating a tree in years," Tanner confessed quietly.

Kyla turned toward him, assuming that he was just joking, but he was staring at the Christmas tree in awe, as if surprised he'd had a part in making a thing like that happen. She was feeling rather surprised herself. This stranger, this man who most likely wouldn't be in her life very long at all, was making her feel emotions that were changing her universe. He was making her forget her sadness, if only for a moment in time.

"It's so beautiful," she said. But she was barely able to focus on the tree instead of on him.

And Tanner made it impossible. He was now looking straight at her, and she couldn't help but return the favor when she felt the burning of those amazing eyes. And she suddenly found herself on the verge of tears and in desperate need of retreat.

He noticed, of course.

"What's the matter, Kyla?"

"I should really get going. It's late." She knew she was running, but she didn't care.

Tanner was instantly in front of her face. "Why are you always in such a hurry to leave as soon as the temperature rises a few degrees or we begin to talk about emotions?" He wrapped his arms behind her back and tugged her against his chest — the beautiful chest she'd been hyperventilating over earlier.

"Because I know what's happening, Tanner." She couldn't help but give him an honest answer.

"And what is that?"

"You want me in your bed." Why not put it out there? Why not get the focus off her emotions? That was more like it.

"Yes, I do." It was hardly an earth-shaking admission.

"Well, then, you should know that it isn't going to happen," she said, her voice slightly breathless.

"Challenge accepted," he told her with a smile, pushing his hips against hers and letting her feel the effect she had on him.

Her blood heated, her body softened, and her knees grew weak. She was so lucky to b sitting down. This man's voice was seductive and his body was hard. She could see why he was so confident in succeeding with her. At least she didn't feel on the verge of tears anymore.

"Take it any way you want, Tanner, just as long as you know it's never going to happen," she said, and she twisted out of his arms. If she decided to play games with this man, he'd be the only winner.

"Mmm, I'd love to take *you* any way I want. I have lots of

ways I've been planning on taking you."

Gosh, he was making her melt. To be desired by such a god of a man was quite the esteem builder. Would it really be so bad to allow herself some pleasure, just a little measure of it? No, it wouldn't. The way she'd feel the next morning was what she dreaded. She'd never been one of those women who could give her body freely. There had to be something beyond simple sensation — there had to be emotions involved that didn't come down to unmitigated lust.

Leaning back into him, she initiated a kiss for the first time, allowing herself to savor him for several moments. She could feel that he was surprised, but he didn't waste any time in pulling her even more closely against him as he ravished her mouth.

When she felt herself falling over the edge of sanity, she pushed off against his chest.

"I just wanted another taste," she said, then tugged against his hold.

Why was she disappointed when he let her go without a struggle? This was what she wanted, she reminded herself.

"Have a great night, Tanner," she said steadily. And she walked to his door and opened it.

He followed her outside and watched while she unlocked her door and went inside.

The last thing she saw before firmly shutting the door between them was his unblinking eyes. He was sending her a clear message: *This is in no way finished.*

CHAPTER FOURTEEN

"ARE YOU READY for work?"

Kyla stood in her doorway, trying to wipe the sleep from her eyes. "What are you talking about?"

"It's time for work. We're going to the same place, so why not go together?"

Tanner was standing in her doorway and looking far too handsome and much too perky for so early in the morning. Granted, it was nine in the morning, but still, she'd been up late, so that equaled too early to be so happy while standing in her doorway. Working two jobs this holiday season had seemed like a good idea at the time, but not when it meant she was giving up sleep, blessed sleep, for just a few extra dollars.

"I'm not ready," she told him.

"That's all right. I'll wait." Then, before she even invited him in, he pushed past the door and waltzed into her apartment.

Kyla stood there for a moment longer as she surveyed her raggedy space with utter embarrassment. Sure, she'd done the best she could on her tight budget, but the furniture was secondhand and there weren't many decorations to speak of. Plain and drab.

He looked out of place in her apartment, though he was residing in the same building. Somehow she knew he didn't belong there, though. She wasn't sure how; his clothes weren't that out of the ordinary. But he clearly wasn't the type of man who lived in a low-end complex like this one — no. He was the type who lived in a sky-rise and looked down upon the city. She didn't know that for sure, but it was just the way he carried himself. An air about him, perhaps.

"I...um...I guess, have a seat," she finally muttered as she tugged on her shirt and shuffled past him in her fluffy slippers.

He'd come at a perfect time. She was wearing an old pair of sweats and a ten-year-old T-shirt, her preferred sleeping attire. Sleeping was about comfort, not fashion. But she'd hardly been expecting her incredibly hot neighbor to show up before she'd even managed to climb out from her bed.

Rushing into her bedroom, she gathered clothes, then snuck into the only bathroom in the apartment and turned the shower on as hot as the dang thing would go. It felt strange to take a shower while knowing Tanner was virtually on the other side of the door. Yep, her apartment was that minuscule.

As the water cascaded down her body, her nipples tightened and a shiver ran through her. What would she do if he strode into the room, drew open the shower curtain without a qualm, then climbed inside with her and pinned her to the wall?

She'd probably attack him, that's what she would do. And why? She didn't know this man, had only had a few conversations with him. She'd never even had a date with the guy. Well, the tree trimming could count as a date if she wanted it to.

The two of them had shared food, wine, and laughter. Oh, and a few hot kisses — she couldn't forget those. But he hadn't asked her out or anything. She'd just shown up with a tree on a whim and then they'd ended up spending the evening together.

Why couldn't she be one of those bold women who just went after what they wanted? Once she emerged from the shower, she wiped the fog off the mirror and analyzed her reflection. She wasn't the most beautiful of women, but she also wasn't exactly ugly.

She took care of her body, and her skin. She didn't spend hours in front of the mirror, but she occasionally liked to fix her hair up nicely and spritz on some perfume. Why did some couples make their relationships seem so easy, while people like her seemed so lost in this whole mess?

Maybe it came down to confidence. Maybe she needed to just forget about what the world expected. Maybe she should just go after what she wanted. The problem with that, though, was that she didn't know what she wanted. At least she hadn't known what it was for the last two years.

All she knew for sure was that Tanner was the first man in ages who had set off a spark inside of her, and she wanted to see where that spark might lead. But she wasn't sure she'd ever have the courage to admit that to him.

With a long-suffering sigh, she pushed away from the mirror and got dressed. She would have to face this man at some point soon. She couldn't hide in her bathroom forever, though the idea wasn't unappealing right now.

When she finally opened the door, a pleasant smell drifted toward her and she followed her nose to the tiny kitchen. She was in shock when she found Tanner standing at her stove with a towel tucked into the front of his jeans and a spatula in hand.

"Hope you're hungry, 'cause I sure am," he said as he flipped a piece of French toast in the frying pan.

"You're cooking?" she said stupidly. Obviously he was.

"I didn't think you would mind. I brought over the stuff from my place, so you're not out any food."

"You brought food over?"

"Are you going to repeat everything I say? With only minor variations, of course." He stopped what he was doing and turned to face her.

"I…uh…"

"Yeah, yeah, I'm a master chef and you're impressed," he said with a big grin.

She paused for another moment before an answering

grin broke out on her face. "I actually *am* impressed," she said before pulling down two plates from her cupboard and setting them at her little table.

"Wow. Didn't expect you to admit that," he told her with a cheesy smile.

"I call it how I see it." Kyla's confusion was evaporating, though she wasn't sure why. She placed the syrup and butter on the table and waited for him to bring the food over.

Why was she spending so much time analyzing this? Hadn't he said he wouldn't be at these apartments very long? Didn't that mean that she really had nothing to risk by flirting with him, by just enjoying his company?

Even if she did end up getting a little attached to the man, he would leave just as quickly as he'd appeared in her life. She didn't yet know if she was willing to sleep with him, but a bit of harmless banter didn't hurt anyone, right?

She took her first bite and then had to gush. "Oh my goodness, this is great. How did you come up with it?"

"This French toast is a sworn secret. There's no way I could divulge the recipe."

"I have ways of making you talk, Tanner."

"By all means, make me," he said with a waggle of his eyebrows.

"This stuff is good enough that I just might try." She didn't even know who she was as she continued flirting with Tanner so shamelessly. She also didn't care. It just felt right.

The two of them finished their meal, and then she insisted on washing the few dishes involved before they left her apartment.

When they entered the street and began strolling along, Kyla was a little bit afraid at the comfortableness she now felt with Tanner. This was certainly a routine she could get used to. When his hand reached for hers and she accepted the twining of their fingers, her heart started to flutter.

Maybe now was the time to worry about getting attached to him. She could certainly feel something when she was with this man, something much more potent than she wanted to admit to.

But for now, she didn't have the time to worry about it. Maybe she would tomorrow. Or maybe the day after tomorrow.

CHAPTER FIFTEEN

Y *EAH, YOU'VE GOT* that something…

That was it! He must be in a freaking time slip, thrown back decades to a silly period when even four grown men sang stupid songs about holding hands.

The whole thing was just weird. He'd started to walk Kyla to and from the mall over the past few days — what if she was followed again? That was a good excuse, wasn't it? And each day, dammit, he took her fingers with his, and his thumb rubbed against her satin skin, and he felt as if he never wanted to let go. What in the hell was he thinking?

This was a new one for him. Who held hands anymore, except maybe old married people? What was the point? Okay, there was a pulse nearby, so maybe if you pushed at it cleverly, it would serve some automotive function and send a babe you wanted into overdrive. He'd have to check that out on the Web.

But sex hadn't been what he was thinking when he lost his hand-holding virginity as a grown man in his thirties. For some reason, he couldn't seem to tear his gaze away from their joined fingers, and couldn't ignore how right it felt.

This woman — a woman, he reminded himself, whom he'd known for a couple of weeks — was starting to dominate his thoughts, even in his sleep. She was quickly getting underneath his skin, and, oddly enough, that didn't terrify him as much as it should.

He should have been running from her as fast as he could, but instead, he found himself seeking her out, offering his help, and enjoying nothing more than her company. So far, all she'd allowed him to do was kiss her.

Hell, he hadn't even managed to get the woman's shirt off yet, and still, he felt content. He'd never worked so hard before to close a deal, and he'd certainly never enjoyed spending so much time in a woman's presence.

In the past he'd grown bored after taking a woman out once or twice. Maybe his fascination with Kyla stemmed from the fact that he hadn't bedded her yet. That had to be it. It really was time that he stop this juvenile madness. He had work to do. It was time to grow up.

But he hadn't seen Kyla all day, and he missed her, missed her tremendously, missed her touch, her voice, her wit, her little jokes. So he found himself walking from his apartment and standing in front of her door.

Damn. More of her cookies and their heavenly smell. Was this planned? Did she know the way to his…stomach?

His hand lifted, made a fist, and rapped on her door, almost against his will. He should go back home — sheesh, was he calling this place *home* now? — but...hell. He knew it was futile even to think that thought. He wanted to see her, wanted to pull her in close for another kiss — even if that's all he was going to get from her.

"I missed you today," he blurted out when her door opened and she appeared, looking scrumptious enough for him to take a bite.

Her hair was tied back, a few escaped tendrils lying softly against her face, and she had flour smeared across her nose and forehead. Wearing an apron that was also covered in flour and had the motto *Cooks do it hotter,* she looked better than if she'd been standing before him in the finest lingerie.

Yeah, he had it bad.

"Invite me in?"

She replied with a lift of her eyebrow and a slight smile on her lips as she waited for him to continue.

"I want to taste your...cookies," he said with a wolfish smile.

Some women might have gotten huffy. Not her. Kyla laughed and, much to his surprise, opened her door wider so he could step through. That was another thing he loved about her, the fact that she could take what he dished out and even give it back most of the time.

"You look so pathetic standing there with drool on your chin; how could I possibly send you away without getting...a taste?"

His heart rate jumping up by at least fifty beats per minute, Tanner couldn't stand it any longer. He cornered her in the kitchen and, without giving her time to resist, pulled her against him as he lowered his head. He had to have a mouthful before he died of hunger.

Kyla didn't hesitate; she lifted her flour-covered hands and clasped his head, kissing him back with a hunger of her own. It was almost as if they were both breaking a long, torturous fast.

Driven almost mad with his desire for her, Tanner lifted her up and set her on the counter, his hips quickly seeking out relief between her thighs. He drew her forward and cradled her sweet, hot core between his legs. He leaned in, needing her to know how desperate he was for her, if she didn't know already.

She tugged on his hair and pressed against him; both of them groaned as their tongues danced. Tanner ran his hand down her back, slipped his fingers beneath the hem of her shirt and moved it upward.

Silk.

That's what her skin felt like — pure silk. He trailed his hand up, caressing the fine muscles of her back, splaying his fingers wide against her flesh. As she whimpered into his mouth, he leaned back just a bit and moved his hand around her rib cage, his thumb brushing the underside of her breast with his thumb.

Yes! Yessssss…

Without further hesitation, he cupped that luscious

mound, feeling her soft skin through the tiny lace bra she was wearing.

Perfect.

She was absolutely perfect, fitting just right in the palm of his hand. He wanted the fabric out of his way, wanted to taste the sweet peaks of her breasts, needed her to be lying beneath him. He reached down, preparing to pull her shirt over her head, when a loud beeping startled him. Kyla edged away, staring at him sightlessly.

"I'm sorry. That got out of hand," she whispered.

Tanner found himself leaning against the counter, his body throbbing as he looked at the space she'd been filling only moments before. Turning toward her, he saw her hands shaking as she pulled a hot pan from the oven and set it on the stovetop.

"Why don't you just turn off the oven so we can continue what we started?" he said, coming up behind her and running his hands down her sides to rest on her hips.

She shuddered in his arms, then bent forward and gripped the front of the stove. Tanner took the opportunity to slide his mouth seductively down the curve of her neck.

"I can't," she said, wriggling out of his embrace and turning around to look at him.

"I don't understand, Kyla." He wasn't going to let her off the hook without an explanation.

"I don't want to have sex, Tanner." She couldn't be any clearer than that. "If you want to leave, I understand."

At first, he had to contend with the slightest edge of

irritation. She was lying. It was more than obvious that she did indeed want to have sex. Why was she fighting him so hard? It wasn't as if either one of them was a virgin. When two people felt a mutual attraction, shouldn't they just do what their bodies were meant to do? Get naked and get it on, right?

"Yes, you do," he finally replied when the silence had stretched on for too long.

"No. I know you probably think I'm nothing but a tease, but I don't want to have sex. I just…"

She trailed off as if she didn't know what she wanted. But he wasn't worried. He knew what she wanted. He could think for the both of them.

He leaned against her, taking her chin with his fingers and lifting her head so she was forced to look at him. "If you want to wait a while longer, I'll wait."

He was bowled over when those words exited his mouth. That hadn't been what he'd intended to say. But when a shocked but grateful expression entered her eyes, he knew he'd said the right thing. He leaned down and kissed her chastely, and then backed up. He absolutely couldn't keep touching her right now or he would quickly have her back up on the counter.

"I brought wine," he said, going back to the door and grabbing the bottle he'd left just inside the door, where he'd hastily set the bottle his assistant had brought to him at his request.

Kyla looked a little unsure, but after a couple of seconds,

she went to her cupboard and pulled out two glasses.

"I don't have fancy wineglasses, but I'm sure it will taste the same no matter what we drink it from," she said with a self-conscious giggle.

"Of course it will," he said, though some experts claimed that the shape of the glass could influence wine's flavor and aroma. No need to point that out. Could he taste or smell anything but her? Not bloody likely. So he poured the wine and asked, "What can I do to help?" He leaned against the counter as she began taking the cookies off the pan and setting them on wax paper.

"You can stay out of the way so I can finish up in here."

"Have you forgotten that I'm a master chef, Kyla?"

"I haven't forgotten that, but this is *my* cooking time, and I don't like to be shown up."

With a grin, Tanner grabbed a couple of the cookies, taking a big bite from one and groaning his approval. "Oh, this is good," he mumbled. Once he'd swallowed, he popped the rest of the cookie in his mouth.

He saw the delight in her eyes at his compliment, and though she scolded him, telling him to quit eating all the cookies, she put a glass of milk in front of him and said he needed it to wash them down. Cookies and wine just didn't have the same flair.

"Who taught you how to bake?" he asked when his mouth was finally empty.

"My mother," she said quietly, and her eyes drooped.

He shouldn't, but he really wanted to know her full story,

know what had happened a couple of years ago. Yes, he could look it up, find out the information from a second party, but that's not what he wanted. He wanted her to tell him, to share with him. She'd given him only a small snippet so far.

"You know you can talk to me about it if you need to."

"Why would you want to listen to my drama?" Kyla was trying to make a joke here, but it was falling flat.

"Sometimes it's easier to talk to someone you don't know real well, someone who wasn't there."

"I may eventually take you up on that offer," she said before pausing. "If you're still around."

She said that last part with a disappointment that lingered, and Tanner suddenly felt himself wanting to be around long enough for her to trust him.

But he wouldn't be. They both knew that. Tanner wasn't the type of man who stayed in the trenches too long. Yes, he'd had his moments in his life when he found himself among the masses, but those times didn't last. There were a couple of kinds of people in this world, and he was certainly on the top of the list.

He didn't know where Kyla stood. Yes, she was down and out right now, but he had a feeling it wasn't a place she would stay too long, either. Did the two of them have more in common than he'd originally thought? She couldn't have the kind of money and influence he had, even with all the billionaires now on the ground, but she could certainly be a powerhouse of her own. But what did all of that matter anyway? The rich bitches he'd known had been just that, really — bitches. Not that he was any prize when it came down to it.

Shaking off the mood-killing thoughts, he popped another cookie in his mouth.

"Let's watch a movie," he said as he watched her take out her last tray of goodies.

"A movie?"

"Haven't I said this before? You really like repeating what I say, Kyla." He chuckled, then stood up and moved over to her DVD stand.

"You just change subjects so quickly and so often that I'm trying to keep up," she told him.

"I like to keep you off kilter. It's fun."

"That's not very nice, Tanner," she told him with a mock glare.

"Baby, I'm all kinds of fun," he replied, snaking his arm around her and tugging her in close to his heated body.

"Tanner," she said in a warning tone, but her breathing had already accelerated and he hadn't even kissed her yet.

"I'll break down your walls, sweetheart; you can trust me on that." Tanner's mouth moved dangerously close to hers. He felt immense satisfaction when her eyes widened. "But I'll be good for now. Okay, not as good as I could be…"

With that, he released her and picked out a DVD, not even caring what it was as the two of them sat on her couch to watch the flick.

"This is my favorite one," she said as *It's a Wonderful Life* began playing.

He rolled his eyes. "I've never understood why everyone loves this movie so much. His life is completely destroyed."

"That's the point, Tanner. He has to see what effect taking his own life could have on those he loves. Before that happens, he can't truly appreciate the good of what he is and what he does."

Although he disagreed with her interpretation and still hated the film, Tanner shut up and watched the movie with her. As it continued to play, he scooted closer and closer to her on the couch, draped his arm around her, and began stroking her neck. But he kept his eyes focused on the TV.

She was a bit stiff at first, but she soon relaxed, raising her hand to rest on his chest. Then she snuggled closer and sighed at parts of the movie she particularly liked.

When the movie ended, Tanner looked down and noticed that she was so relaxed, in fact, that she'd fallen asleep in his arms. Carefully cradling her to him, he lifted her up and proceeded down the short hallway to what was obviously her bedroom.

He managed to pull back a handmade quilt while still holding her, and then laid her down on the soft sheets. After covering her up, he stared down at her face, so beautiful and at peace.

Turning and walking away – God, it was hard — he switched off her lights and made sure her front door was locked. Now this was frightening. In less than three weeks, this woman had become more than just a conquest to him.

The question was, what did he want to do about that?

When he stepped back inside his apartment, feeling pretty great, if still confused, his foot suddenly slipped out from beneath him and he went flying into the air, a resounding *oof* coming from his lungs as he landed hard enough to knock the wind out of him. Once he caught his breath, he realized he was flat on his back and in at least two inches of water. If he'd been paying attention, he would have noticed the water leaking out into the hallway.

Jumping up and feeling a nasty ache run down his back, he sloshed his way through the water and made it into his kitchen, where he could hear the distinct sound of gushing. When he opened the cupboard below the sink, he was immediately sprayed in the face. He jumped back and found himself staring at a burst pipe.

He was drenched by the time he located the shutoff valve, and the language he was using about this building and all its problems wouldn't have gone over well with the cute little kiddies at the mall. This was hell, pure damnation, and suddenly the rest of his sentence in this building seemed like it would stretch an eternity.

He snatched up his phone and woke his assistant up to demand that a plumber be sent over right freaking now. This was going to cost him a fortune. Because of the judge's orders, now that he had to repair the pipes in his own worthless apartment, it looked as if the entire building would be getting new ones too.

When he called the police to explain that he needed to change apartments, they were less than sympathetic, offering to bring him a pair of hip waders. After slamming down the phone, Tanner sloshed to his bedroom, his good mood long forgotten as he prepared himself for a "holiday" week without even a remote chance of comfort or joy.

CHAPTER SIXTEEN

ARE YOU FREAKING kidding me?"

With the light from his phone, Tanner had finally found a flashlight, and he flipped it on. Then he went back to cursing into his cell. He was barely able to hear the voice on the other end past the rushing sound in his ears; it was born of pure fury. "What do you mean, there's nothing you can do? If I say get down here, I mean it!"

The person at the other end of the line continued speaking but was absolutely no help whatsoever. Slamming the phone's End button as hard as he could, Tanner dropped the device on the counter and ran his hand through his hair.

"How in the hell does anyone tolerate this damn building?" he shouted into the air. Yes, he knew he sounded like a crazy person, but if it wasn't one problem then it was another. His pipes had burst, mice ran around rampant, and now the damn electricity was out.

The guy said it was most likely a breaker, that too many circuits were being used now that the heating was back on. They couldn't come in until the next day. Of course they couldn't. And it was going to be a major expense, another one, to update the wiring of the building and bring the electrical boxes up to code.

Why did he give a flying whatever? He should just let the tenants live in darkness. Then maybe they'd take a hint at long last and finally leave so he could hire that bulldozer to come in. At this point, he would sit on the ball while it smashed through the walls. The injuries to his body would be worth it — he'd be feeling the damn building crumble beneath his feet.

"Tanner?"

Stopping his pacing, he shined his light over toward his front door, where Kyla was standing, shifting on her feet and looking nervous.

"What?" he growled, and when she flinched, he felt immediately ashamed of himself. "I'm sorry, Kyla. I'm just frustrated."

"It's okay," she told him as she stepped inside. "I knocked, but I don't think you heard, so I tried the knob and it was open and…" She was fighting to control her voice. "It's just that the dark sort of freaks me out."

"What? It's the same place, just a little…darker. And anyway, you have a flashlight, too." He moved toward her now, until they were standing right there together, facing each other.

"I know that logically, Tanner, but it doesn't help much. I don't like not being able to see who or what is around — me except for in this stupid, narrow beam of light."

"In this damn place, who knows what that might be?" he said without thinking, and he felt the shudder pass through her body. "Sorry," he said again, and this time he was mumbling.

"No. It's true. Bad things can happen in the dark," she said, edging a couple of inches closer. She was practically pressed against him now.

His bad mood quickly deflated. How could he be angry when her warm body was next to his?

"I know the breaker box is in the basement, Tanner. I… uh…just don't want to go down there by myself. I mean, someone else might be thinking the same thing, but then again, everyone might be thinking everyone else is going to go down there." That rush of words was almost amusing.

"Breaker box? Do you even know what to do with one?"

"I'm not some simpering female that doesn't even know how to flip a switch up and down," she snapped.

Tanner had to smile. "Okay, that was an asinine question. Why don't we go check it out and see if we can do anything about this darkness?" He held out his arm.

It took her a few moments — she was obviously still irritated with him — but her fear of the dark outweighed her irritation, and she finally gave in. They left his apartment and made their way toward the service door that led to the basement.

"Where in the hell is security? Shouldn't they be the ones doing this?" Tanner asked as they opened the door and faced a set of stairs that he didn't trust to hold their weight.

"I don't think this is in their job description. Besides, one of the guards, the one that works mostly nights, kind of gives me the creeps."

Tanner stopped moving and turned toward her. Their flashlights were shining downward, though, and he couldn't see her face. Talk about frustrating.

But he tried to sound calm. "How so?" he asked.

"I don't know. He just seems…oh, I'm being stupid. I'm sure there's nothing at all wrong with him. I just get the creeps around him. No reason," she said quietly, obviously focused on the staircase in front of her.

"Let me know if anything weird happens." Was it all in her head? That wasn't unlikely, but still, people usually got a feeling, whether good or bad, for a reason.

"I'm sure it's nothing. Are we both stalling on going down these steps, or is it my imagination?" she asked with a nervous laugh.

"Fine. You caught me. I think I would just about rather do anything other than go down these stairs. Isn't this how all good horror movies start or end, and aren't the people watching the flicks the ones shouting at the television, telling the characters to turn around and run like hell?"

Kyla's body shook, and he was worried for a moment before she erupted in a big laugh. "I cannot believe you just said that, Tanner. You sound just like a frightened little girl right now," she managed to gasp out between bursts of laughter.

"Hey. I'm a damn superhero. I'm going into the basement, aren't I?" he said a bit indignantly.

"Yes, you're my rock, big boy," she told him, and then she moved forward, leaving him no choice but to accompany her down the stairs.

Tanner was terrified that if so much as a bug rushed across him, he would end up screaming just like that little girl she'd just mentioned. If he did that, he'd never be able to face this woman again. And dammit, he wanted sex and he wanted it soon, so the bugs had better stay far away from him.

Of course the stairs creaked as the two made their way down them, and he heard scratching from some unknown place down in the dark basement — of course. But there was no way he was frightened. He was just worried about her. After all, she was pressed beside him and he couldn't help but feel the tremors racking her body. He didn't think the shaking now had anything to do with mirth. The creepiness of the basement was freaking her out.

"If you want to wait up top, I can deal with this." He enjoyed having her cling to his side, but he had to make the suggestion.

"No way am I waiting up there all by myself. I know how this works. It's always the girl who gets killed first."

Her serious tone broke the last of Tanner's tension. How could he be nervous when she was so dead set on imagining the two of them in a horror movie. Yeah, he'd been the one to mention it first, but she was the one acting it out now. He began to chuckle and then he outright laughed, the sound echoing off the walls of the dingy basement.

"This is so not funny, Tanner, and I think you're being very rude right now," she said, though they both knew it *was* sort of funny.

"I know it isn't exactly funny, Kyla, but look at us. We're slowly descending into a basement, nothing worse, and both of us are being ridiculous about it. No monsters are going to jump out and get us."

"Maybe not all monsters are imaginary."

"Believe me, Kyla, I know that," he said. All of earlier humor was now gone.

They did live in a world where the real monsters weren't green or purple, ghouls, mutants, aliens, or the dead or undead — these monsters had dark souls lived among the people unnoticed. They didn't care about humanity and they didn't care about hurting others. They were the monsters everyone really had to fear.

He pulled Kyla just a little bit closer. When they arrived at the basement floor, Tanner shined the light around until he found the large breaker box in a dusty corner, surrounded by gigantic cardboard boxes that had who knew what in them.

What with the cobwebs hanging off those boxes and off rusty metal furniture, and the shadows cast by their flashlights, it seemed a perfect setting for something terrifying to happen. Even the creaking of the old floorboards down here added to the spooky atmosphere. Tanner was determined to trudge ahead though. They made their way toward the circuit breakers, and it took them a while to pull the rusty door open, but when they did, what was before them wasn't helpful at all.

A lot of the switches were broken, and nothing was labeled. Yes, there was a main breaker, but it was so rusted, Tanner was afraid that if he so much as touched it, the thing would snap off and electrocute them both.

He shined his flashlight on the breaker box for a good few minutes, and then sighed heavily. "I think this was a wasted trip. There's absolutely nothing we're going to be able to do with this."

"That's what I was thinking too," Kyla had to say, "but I hate to leave all of these people without power. It's so cold out, and now people won't even be able to shower."

"I know. This really does suck, but it looks like we'll have to wait until the maintenance guys come in."

"If they ever do. I don't know who owns this building, but the corporation doesn't have a conscience at all. Look how long it took to get the heat back on, and we only recently started getting our pipes fixed. If it isn't one thing here, then it's another."

Her grousing made him feel about two inches tall.

"I'm sorry, Kyla."

"Why are you sorry? It's not your fault, Tanner, and you know it. You should be just as irritated as I am, even if you aren't staying here very long. We have basic rights as humans, you know? Like a safe and warm place to sleep, especially if we're paying rent."

Tanner wanted to tell her again that he was sorry, wanted to tell her he would make sure everything was fixed, but he wasn't planning to do that. No. He was planning to see that she and the rest of the remaining tenants evacuated this old building, and then rip the old place down.

And he wasn't going to lie to himself. The new apartments would go for five times the rent that these ones did. None of the tenants here would be able to afford to live in the new complex. Did he feel a twinge of guilt for the first time? Maybe.

But wasn't it money that made the world go round? It did to him and to a lot of people. The saying about love was so much garbage. Yes, his set of fancy condos would cost a lot more money for its new residents, but why should that bother him? He was also going to boost the economy here. Think about the construction jobs, a lot of them, and business opportunities, too — there would be a mini-mall inside the complex, dammit. That made him less of a monster, didn't it?

When they turned to leave, they heard a loud shuffling from behind the staircase. Tanner automatically pushed Kyla behind him as he shined the light in that direction.

"What was that?" she asked, her voice trembling. "It sounds a heck of a lot bigger than a rat scurrying across the floor."

Before he could say anything, there was a scratching

sound like someone moving, and Tanner was now absolutely certain that they weren't alone. Maybe their horror flick scenario had just come true.

Tanner refused to let Kyla come up beside him as he moved toward the sound. What he should do was try to rush up the stairs and bolt the door closed. But, hell, if they were in a horror flick, they might as well be the stupid fools who walked straight to their deaths. No use ruining a standard plot. Besides, what if someone else had come down the stairs to try to fix the problem and had fallen and was just now waking up?

Just as he and Kyla reached the edge of the stairs, their flashlights pointed at the dark area beneath, a blood-curdling scream ripped through the air.

CHAPTER SEVENTEEN

KYLA WAS ON Tanner's back with her legs wrapped around him before she knew what she was doing. When he said something and his voice came out indistinct, she vaguely realized that her hands were around his throat, most likely cutting off his lower airway. The problem was that she couldn't make her muscles unclench. She told herself to let go, but it just wasn't going to happen. She was a helpless mass of terror.

"Can't breathe, Kyla," Tanner choked out.

"Wh…wh…what was that?" That was all she finally managed to get through her chattering teeth.

"Let go and I'll find out. I don't want to hurt you by prying your hands away," he wheezed.

Somehow she managed to loosen her grip around his neck, but nothing she tried was allowing her legs to give up their hold on his waist. She wasn't going to move from his back.

"Okay, you have to climb down, Kyla, so I can figure this out," he said, his voice still a bit hoarse, but sounding better than it had when she was nearly throttling him.

"Nope. Not letting go," she told him.

To her amazement, a small chuckle escaped his raw throat. "Okay." He moved forward and spoke to whatever monster was threatening them. "Who is there? I'm not going to hurt you unless I have to," he said.

Whoa. Tanner really sounded frightening now Kyla wouldn't want to be on this man's bad side.

There was more shuffling behind the stairs, and she was really shaking now. This was it. They were both going to die because they were the stupid ones who had willingly — well, okay, not quite willingly — gone down into the dark and dingy basement.

"Listen up," Tanner said. "Come out now or I start shooting."

That stopped Kyla's fidgeting. He didn't have a gun — or at least she didn't think he had a gun. She wasn't going to question him, though, because if the intruder assumed he had a gun, then maybe he, she, or it wouldn't try to go after them with a bloody hatchet.

They heard even more shuffling, and then Tanner backed up a few paces and turned his light once more in the direction of the sound. After a few more tense seconds, she saw dirty blond hair, and then a small body. It rose slowly and walked toward them.

"Please don't hurt me," the voice quavered.

Tanner froze as a child walked toward them.

Kyla barely recognized the boy, and it took her a few moments to place him with all the dirt on his face. "Billy?" she finally said.

"Yes, ma'am," he replied. He came up to them, trembling.

"What are you doing down here?" Tanner asked. He knelt on the ground, quite a feat because Kyla was still attached to him.

That was the point she realized that she needed to let him go. She carefully untwined her limbs from his body and landed on her rear with a slight thump. She stood up slowly and staggered away from him so she could find the flashlight she'd dropped. Any movement at all was now difficult; she felt an ache all through her because she'd been wound around him so tightly. She wondered whether he had bruises where her legs had held him in a death grip.

"I'm hiding," Billy said.

Why in the world would he be hiding? There were so many questions Kyla wanted to ask him, but she knew they needed to get out of this creepy basement first. When she discovered her flashlight, she turned back to him and Tanner, and then spoke.

"Let's go upstairs and you can talk to us." When she came closer again, it broke her heart to see that the boy's cheeks were sunken, and dark circles were prominent under his five-year-old eyes.

Billy didn't argue when she took his ice-cold hand in hers

and turned him around so they could make their way up the staircase. She knew Tanner would follow. She went down the hallway and straight to her apartment. Once inside, she lit the candles she already had sitting out. They cast a dim glow on the room, and she took the time to get a really good look at Billy's face.

It was covered in dirt and he looked exhausted and sad. What was going on?

"Billy, why were you in the basement, and why are you so dirty?" She sat him down on a chair and then went over to her kitchen sink. She didn't have hot water, but she could at least wipe some of the grime off his face.

After trying to warm the cloth up in her hands as much as possible before touching it to his skin, she walked up to him and began wiping him down. He flinched at the contact but didn't try to stop her.

"Look, Billy, you have to tell us why you were down there," Kyla said when she'd finished cleaning him up. "I'm sure your grandmother is worried sick about you."

His eyes filled with tears, and when they spilled over, Kyla felt her own eyes begin to sting. Tanner took that moment to come into her apartment, a soda and some crackers in his hands, and he joined Billy at the table, popped the tab on the soda, and slid it in front of the boy. Billy didn't even look at it.

"I've been bad," he said on a sob that tore into Kyla's heart.

She tried to reassure him. "Oh, Billy, you couldn't have

done anything very wrong."

"I hurt my grandma," he choked out.

Kyla was stunned by those words, and she had no earthly idea how to respond. It certainly wasn't what she'd been expecting the young child to say.

"How did you hurt your grandma?" Tanner asked as he pushed the soda a little closer. "Why don't you have a drink first before telling us all about it? You don't want your throat to hurt if you talk too much."

Billy took the can obediently and swallowed a small amount before putting the soda down and looking over at Tanner. More tears were falling down the boy's newly cleaned face.

"Grandma always tells me to pick up my toys, and sometimes — well, most of the time — I forget, 'cause I just do. I don't know why. I left my car in the hallway and grandma came out of her room and she fell over it. She hit her head and then I couldn't wake her up. I called the 911 number she told me about and then I hid. I didn't want them to take me away 'cause I hurt my grandma." He started to sob, and his tiny body shook.

"Oh, Billy. You didn't do anything wrong," Kyla said, feeling so much pain for this poor child. "Your grandma isn't mad at you." She just prayed that Vivian was all right. She made eye contact with Tanner, who was already lifting his phone to dial security. How had they not noticed Billy when he went down to the basement?

"How long were you down there, sweetie?" Kyla asked.

"I don't know. I fell asleep, and when I woke up, it was really dark and I was scared, but I didn't know what to do."

Tanner spoke quickly to Kyla. "His grandma was transported last night to the hospital a few blocks down the road. Let me make one more call and then we can take him down there."

He stepped from the room and made whatever call he needed to make, and then he came back in. "Okay, it's all good. We can go," he said.

She was thoroughly confused. It sounded as if Tanner needed to get permission to go to the hospital, but that made no sense. So maybe that wasn't the call he'd mentioned. Of course it wasn't.

They blew out the candles, left Kyla's apartment, and by some miracle managed to hail a cab to take them to the hospital. Tanner had phoned for one, but he didn't want to wait. When they reached the hospital room of Billy's grandmother, Kyla had to fight back tears again. The poor woman had so many wires hooked up to her.

The next hour flew quickly. They weren't able to get a lot of information, but what they learned was that she was in a coma from her fall to the floor, and that her hip had been broken. Kyla and Tanner waited in a quiet room nearby, and soon someone from Children's Protective Services showed up.

"Billy, we're going to need you to come with us," the woman said after she introduced herself.

"Because I was bad," Billy said in a rocky voice, his

shoulders hunched as his small fingers clung to Kyla's.

"No, Billy, not because you were bad, but because your grandma is sick right now and can't take care of you," the woman told him. "We're going to take you to a nice, safe house, a place for you to get comfortable for a little while."

"Why can't he just stay with me?" Kyla asked before she even thought about stopping herself.

"We can't just let the child go with anyone," the woman said, her eyebrows going down in disapproval.

"I live in same apartment building he does, and he's obviously comfortable with me," Kyla argued. "Please let me take him; he'll be closer to home."

"The system doesn't work like that, ma'am, and I would appreciate it if you didn't upset the child any more than he already is," the woman said, and she reached for Billy. "I am sorry. I know you're trying to help him, but this isn't the way to do it. If you contact our offices tomorrow, you can speak with someone about the proper procedures on what you can do to be a foster parent."

Billy clung even more tightly to Kyla. "No, please don't let them take me," he pleaded.

The way he looked up at Kyla made her feel absolutely terrible.

"Billy, I'm going to talk to whoever I need to talk to, okay? I will try to get you as soon as I can, and you'll be with me until your grandma gets better." Kyla spoke carefully, unwilling to let him know that her heart was breaking.

The woman gave them a few more moments and then had

to take the boy away by his arms when he refused again to go with her. "I'm sorry," she said again as the two of them exited the room. Billy was sobbing uncontrollably.

"There was nothing she could have done, Kyla. The law is the law," Tanner said as he wrapped an arm around her shoulders.

"I know, Tanner, but I just feel so bad for the little boy." Her own tears were finally starting to fall despite all her efforts to hold them back.

"Let's go back home, Kyla. We can't do anything for anyone here." He rose to his feet and helped her up from where she'd been kneeling on the floor in front of little Billy.

Kyla didn't have the energy to speak anymore, so she just followed the man out of the room. This night had drained her, and all she wanted to do was lie down and have a good cry. But as she clung to Tanner, she realized she didn't want to do that alone.

CHAPTER EIGHTEEN

SADNESS WEIGHED HEAVILY on Tanner's shoulders, but as he walked into the apartment complex with Kyla at his side, he tried to shake it off. The boy had nothing to do with him and shouldn't influence his moods, but twice now he had seen fear and pain in Billy's eyes and he didn't think it would be all that easy to forget about this kid.

"Can I come to your apartment? I don't want to be alone."

Kyla had whispered those words from her beautiful lips, but they came across so loud and clear that she might as well have shouted them. And they stopped Tanner in his tracks. As her hand clung to his arm, and her body leaned into his, he knew what she was saying, what she was offering.

He also knew it would be wrong for him to take advantage of this situation. She was afraid of the dark, for goodness sake, and even worse, her emotions were frayed because of poor little Billy. He would be the lowest of low if he took her to his bed tonight.

But the thought of doing just that had him instantly forgetting his worries about the building, about the child, about everything bad in his life. Two soft sentences from Kyla and it was taking all his restraint to keep from picking her up in his arms and leading her straight to her bed.

"Why don't we go to your place, Kyla, and I can stay with you until you fall asleep?" He really wanted to punch himself in the mouth for even offering such a thing, but what else could he say if he hoped to be able to live with himself after he left this building for good.

"I don't want to be in my place. I don't want you to leave me alone," she told him, her body trembling against his.

He sent up a silent prayer for strength.

"I won't leave you, then." The words had barely made it past his teeth and he was close to shaking himself.

"I just need to grab a few things, Tanner, and then we can go to your place." She didn't release his arm.

"You really don't want to stay in your apartment tonight, do you?" What were her motives? If he was there with her, she wouldn't be alone. "Anyway, I wouldn't leave you."

"Oh, I think you'll leave. But that's not the point right now."

Well, that was honest enough. And she was probably right. He was a man, and he had only so much willpower. He was glad he hadn't said that out loud. He sounded like a creep even in his own head.

But what could he do? He followed her silently into her apartment. She pulled him to her room and grabbed a few items from her dresser, and then moved back toward her front door.

Tanner was so nervous now that he fumbled with his keys, but he somehow managed to get his apartment door open, and when he headed in, Kyla was still locked against him, so they had to turn sideways to get through.

"I'm not going to leave you — I promise," he said when she still didn't release him.

She let out a nervous chuckle, and she finally loosened her tight grip on him and then dropped her hand. "I'm sorry, Tanner. It's just been a really bad night."

He grabbed her shoulders and pulled her in for a hug. "Don't ever apologize for needing someone," he said as he held her close for several moments.

After leading her to the couch, he left her with a flashlight while he dug for candles, thankful his assistant thought of everything. Yep, Randy was definitely getting that raise now.

The emergency candles cast a strong enough light in the room that Tanner was able to turn off his flashlight without making Kyla more nervous than she already was.

"I put a candle in the bathroom and one in the bedroom so you can move around the apartment without freaking out," he said as he joined her on the couch.

"I know that to be afraid of the dark at my age is ridiculous, but my fear is what it is," she told him, and she snuggled against him.

"I think you're charming, Kyla. You know that no one is perfect, right? No one. Promise not to tell anyone, but even *I'm* not perfect," he said with a chuckle.

She relaxed into his side, and Tanner felt his body instantly harden. No! He tried to control himself, tried telling himself that just because she needed him to comfort her did not give him the right to take unfair advantage.

But here was the thing. Tanner was feeling just as raw as Kyla was and he would love to sink deep inside her heat, love to lose himself inside her for a few sweet hours. He would love to think of nothing beyond the needs of his body and hers, and he'd love to not be reminded how dark the world could actually be.

How was he able to keep from sliding his hands around her and cupping her breasts? Damned if he knew. He simply held her and didn't even think about the time he was wasting doing absolutely nothing.

"Tanner?"

He tensed at the breathless quality of her voice. Everything about this woman screamed "Take me." and he *wanted* to take her.

"Yes?"

"I'm really tired now."

His heart thudded in his chest. She hadn't asked him to make love to her. She'd simply said she was tired. She'd also said she didn't want to be alone. Just because she didn't want to sleep alone didn't guarantee he was going to get sex. It most likely meant that she was going to sleep and he was going to hold her. And he'd be throbbing the whole time.

"Do you want to go to bed?" He barely recognized his own voice.

She was silent for a few heart-stopping moments. "Yes." Her voice was almost inaudible, but not to him. "I need to use your bathroom first. I feel filthy."

"There's no hot water," he reminded her.

"I know. But if you have a washcloth…"

"I can get that for you."

Tanner untangled himself from her arms and then moved to the bathroom, where he laid out a towel and washcloth and picked up the dirty underwear he'd flung in the corner earlier in the day. In his defense, he told himself, he hadn't been expecting a guest.

"The bathroom is ready," he said, making her jump. "Sorry."

"I'm sorry, Tanner. I just…" Again she stopped, and then her sweet lips turned up a fraction of an inch and she stood up and walked toward him. "Thank you. Really. You are too good to me and I don't know why, but you are."

She took his breath away when she leaned against him and brushed her lips lightly across his. Before he was able to grab her, pull her tightly against him and lose complete control, she stepped back and then walked into the bathroom.

He nearly had a stroke when she left the bathroom door open a few inches and he could see her shadow flickering on the wall. Moving quickly away from the temptation — he wasn't a Peeping Tom, dammit — he headed to his bedroom and decided to light another candle. Then he found himself sitting on the edge of the bed.

Should he change? Climb beneath the covers? What was she expecting from him? What was he expecting from himself?

It was cold in his apartment, but as he listened to the sound of water running in his bathroom, he felt a nervous sweat break out on his skin because he wasn't sure if he was going to be able to be strong enough to last with her beside him all night.

When what felt like an hour passed, but was probably just five or ten minutes, he almost jumped at the sound of his own voice. "Are you okay in there?"

When there wasn't an answer, he stood up, moved toward the bathroom door and tapped on it. "Kyla, are you okay?"

"I'm fine. Give me another minute" came her reply and he could hear her nerves loud and clear. They were definitely both feeling the sizzling atmosphere.

Why was he nervous? Why should either of them be nervous? They were adults. They weren't virgins. Sex was natural, it was needed, it was the one true thing that really made the world go round. So if the two of them burned the sheets to help keep them warm and to make the despair of the night disappear, there was nothing wrong with that.

But were they rushing this? Hell, no. He'd been wanting her in his bed since he met her nearly three weeks ago. It was long overdue — if anyone cared to ask him. So why in the world was he so antsy? He was never nervous about having sex. And if they didn't have sex, he wouldn't perish.

Well, maybe he would.

The candlelight flickered softly, casting a warm glow about the cold room. It was the perfect scene for a night of hot sex. Plus, hadn't someone once told him women preferred candlelight because it made everything seem so much more beautiful, hid flaws and all of that? Not that Kyla had a single flaw on her perfect body. Again, he had to remind himself that she'd just asked not to be alone. She hadn't asked for him to make love to her. A groan of frustration barely missed escaping his throat.

When the creaking of the bathroom door alerted Tanner that she was emerging, he looked up and watched her shadow approach before she made it into the bedroom.

"Wow, this is…beautiful," she said, her voice trembling, her nerves obvious.

"The power is out. We needed more light than we had at first." Sheesh. Talk about belaboring the obvious… Would he win an award for Lame Response of the Year? And why was he in this pathetic state?

"Yeah, I know, but it's still beautiful. I'm sort of enjoying the fact that the power is out right now."

She shifted awkwardly. Maybe not all men would find her stunningly beautiful in a pair of sweats and a sweatshirt, but right now, he couldn't imagine a more perfect woman.

Maybe if they were back at his penthouse suite, she would have emerged in a lace teddy with scented oils caressing her skin, but they were in this dive apartment complex, and he just didn't care. All he cared about was that soon she would be lying next to him. Or on top of him. Hmm…

"Maybe I'm being too irrational, and maybe staying wasn't the smartest idea. I…uh…I'm…" She trailed off and Tanner found himself not being able to breathe, let alone speak. "I mean, I'm a big girl. If I get this frightened of the dark, there's a real problem." She didn't look him in the eyes as she shifted on her feet again.

Oh, heck no. He wasn't going to let her leave. With two quick strides, he was right there in front of her; he pulled her to him and felt the shiver travel down her spine. The last thing he wanted was to let her go, even if that meant a night of suffering for him. Tanner was surprised that he would be willing to do nothing more than hold her. But that didn't mean he wasn't going to try to convince her the two of them could make a hell of a lot of magic if their bodies came together though.

Bending down so his words were a warm breath on her neck, he murmured, "We can keep each other warm."

"I'm scared, Tanner."

"We don't have to do anything you don't want to." He just hoped she'd want to do it *all*. Yes, he would probably end up with permanent damage to what he had beneath the belt, if he'd been wearing one, but she was worth it. And his pain was worth being able to hold her close.

"Are you sure?"

He suddenly had a terrifying thought. "You're…um…not a virgin, are you?"

That made her head come up and she finally looked in his eyes before smiling ruefully. "No. But, to be honest, I'm not very experienced...at all."

"That's okay," he said, relief filling him. The longest this could last was one more week, and he didn't want to be responsible for taking her innocence. When he left this building, he wasn't taking anything with him, especially not another person.

So if they made love tonight, that's all she would get — his body, not his mind, his soul, or his love. He needed to tell her this, but the words were trapped in his throat. This was new. He'd never before had difficulty letting a woman know that he could only give her sex, nothing more. But what if the natural light that shone from her eyes dried up? What if he did take her body and then left her empty? Could he live with that?

She cupped his cheek with a gentle hand and leaned forward, kissing him softly before stepping back. She was lighting him on fire. Who needed a freaking furnace? Without another word, he took her hand and led her to the bed.

"Are you trying to seduce me, Tanner?" she asked with a nervous smile.

"Yes." Why should he lie?

"It may be working," she said, then gave him a look that had his breath rushing from him in excitement.

"Lie down," he almost gasped.

She hesitated only a moment before stretching out on his

bed a bit stiffly, her clothes still in place. Tanner picked up the oil he had on the nightstand and rubbed some into his hands to warm it up, and he joined her on the bed.

Sliding his hands beneath the hem of her sweatshirt, he caressed the silk skin of her back — or was it satin? — and when he heard her involuntary moan of approval, his body went from merely ready for action to pulsing, and it took only an instant.

"Are you warm enough?" he asked as his hand moved farther up, pushing up the sweatshirt and exposing her lower back to him. He wanted to see more.

"Yes," she sighed.

Taking a handful of the stupid shirt, he began tugging it upward in earnest, holding his breath, hoping she wouldn't stop him. She lifted her body, making it easier for him to get the material over her head. Then she lay back down, her back to him. Unclasping her bra, he drew the straps down her arms, realizing that his fingers were trembling.

She said nothing as he pulled the lacy material free and tossed it aside. Adding more oil to his hands, he ran his fingers across her back and sides, kneading her muscles as she gave him gasps of pleasure in return.

"Your skin is flawless," he told her.

"Mmm…your hands are magic," she replied, making him smile.

After devoting a good amount of time to her back, he reached into the waistband of her sweatpants and began slowly helping her out of them. Her body tensed, but only for a moment, and then she relaxed again as his hands glided down her legs.

As she lay naked before him, her sweet buttocks looking up at him, Tanner wanted nothing more than to strip off his own clothes, turn her over onto her back, and then plunge deep within her heat. But tonight was about seduction, and it was about pleasure. There was no hurry. He refused to shortchange either of them.

The glow from the candles cast shadows on her skin as he ran his hands over every inch of her. Shivers traveled down her body.

"If you are too cold, I can cover you," he said. "Though it would be a sin to hide your beauty."

"I'm not cold," she sighed. "I'm actually burning up."

Finally, he pushed against her to turn her up toward him. He needed to be face to face with her, to see the glories of her chest and, yes, below. He wasn't sure if she would let that happen — if she did, they both knew what would come next. He was throbbing so consistently that he didn't know how much restraint he'd be able to show her.

But she went along with what he wanted and looked at him through half-closed lids, and it was now his turn to groan in pleasure. Her body was perfect, stunning, in fact — her breasts were high and firm, her stomach curved subtly and beautifully, and then lower, her womanhood positively gleamed, and he was desperate to spread her thighs and taste her.

Instead, he ran his hands up her stomach, the oil coating

her skin as he pushed over the mounds of those amazing breasts and massaged them in his hands. Her nipples jutted out at him imploringly, and her breathing deepened.

"I want you so much, Kyla. This massage can end right now…or we can continue," he said, needing her to understand her choices.

"I want you, too, Tanner," she whispered.

Leaning down, he placed his hands beneath her and pressed her naked body against his clothed one — though, despite those annoying clothes, his hardened manhood was more than apparent. And then he kissed her, a slow, sure kiss that made everything spin.

Tanner's heart thudded in his chest. He slowly moved his mouth down her throat, sucking on her glistening skin as he made his way toward her breasts. The first taste of her sweet nipple stole his breath away, and her groan made him push against her in a desperate attempt to relieve some of the ache in his throbbing shaft.

"So good," he murmured, sucking one nipple into his mouth and flicking it with his tongue before kissing between her breasts and then giving ample attention to her other compelling areola.

Sitting up, Tanner ripped off his shirt, wanting to feel skin against skin. Then, he yanked off his pants, leaving them both naked on the bed together — naked, that was, except for his ever-present thick socks. Their bodies were entwined, their breathing heavy.

"Protection. I forgot protection," he said, knowing he was

now going to wither away to nothing. Or else break apart in a gigantic fireball.

She hesitated for a moment before speaking. "I'm… um…protected. I'm on birth control…um…to control… um…cramps," she told him, her cheeks glowing with embarrassment.

"Good enough for me," he told her. Say what? He'd never said anything like that before. He never trusted women when they claimed they were protected. But he didn't think it was possible not to make love to her right now, so he banished the thought of entrapment from his mind.

He kissed her again, much less gently this time. He devoured her mouth, drinking in her sounds of pleasure once again. And then he moved down her body, pressing his lips to the curve of her stomach before spreading open her thighs and gazing at her delectable womanhood.

"So beautiful," he said reverently before bending forward and swiping his tongue along her heat, her intoxicating scent seeping into his central nervous system and sending him into overdrive.

Slipping his fingers inside her while his tongue explored her slick folds, he groaned against her. She was more than ready for him and he knew he could take her right now. But he didn't want to. He wanted to taste her, feel her, make love to her all night with his mouth alone.

When he felt her body tense, he sucked harder on her swollen bud of pleasure — it was as erect as he was! — and she unleashed a delicious cry that almost echoed through the room as her body shook in ecstasy. A few more gentle flicks from his tongue had her nearly sobbing, and then he climbed back up her body. *Now* he would plunge inside her!

Kyla had other plans, however. Sitting up, she pushed him over onto his back and straddled him, her eyes blazing, the heat from her core warming his pulsing arousal — as if it needed more warmth. Leaning forward, she kissed him, and then she lowered her head and trailed kisses down his chest and over his stomach.

"I've always thought this small patch of hair is so sexy on a man," Kyla said as she kissed his lower stomach, causing it to quiver with her tenderly attentive touch.

He couldn't speak as her lips gave butterfly kisses all down his throbbing staff. When her wonderful fingers gripped him and squeezed, he groaned heavily, his head turning to and fro as he gripped the bedsheets to keep him from grabbing her and flipping her over.

Her tongue circled the head of his arousal before her lips covered him and she sucked him into the hot recesses of her mouth. He felt himself losing control as she explored him, savored him, and pleasured him beyond his wildest dreams.

"No more," he managed to say, just barely. He reached for her and pulled her up his body, keeping her lying on top of him, until they were lined up perfectly for him to thrust upward and join their bodies together.

Wrapping his hands in her hair, he brought her face to his and captured her lips, driving his tongue into her mouth the same way he was about to drive his manhood inside her core.

She squirmed on top of him, her body quivering with her own need, and he guided her thighs further apart with his knees. He reached down to her backside and drew her close so he could rub his arousal on the outside of her heat.

Pushing her upward so she was now in a sitting position, with her legs straddling his body, he watched entranced as the candlelight flickered over her incredible beauty. After running his fingers down her back until he reached her hips, he lifted her up so she was hovering over his arousal, and then he paused.

"Don't close your eyes now," he said as they began to drift shut. "Don't shut me out of your desire. I want to watch you while you feel me slide inside you."

Pushing his hips up at the same time as he pulled her body into him, he felt a rumble of pleasure emerge from his chest and travel up his throat when their bodies finally connected, when her heat surrounded him and she pulsed around him.

"Ohhhh…." She cried out, her eyes on fire, her body shaking.

Tanner couldn't look away as he thrust upward. Kyla quickly caught on and began following his lead in their primitive rhythm, but by no means taking a passive role. They picked up speed, her beautiful breasts bouncing, her skin gleaming.

Trying not to lose control, because he was afraid he might hurt her, Tanner did his damnedest to slow down, but she reached for his shoulders and moaned her disapproval, and then pushed down hard on him.

And he did lose it.

Gripping her hips tightly, he let go and thrust hard in and out of her beautiful heat. Their breathing was manic and their movements grew faster and faster, and then she tensed, and her core gripped him, and gripped him so tight. Her cry of joy and release rent the air. One more deep thrust into her body, and his cry joined hers as he spilled his seed deep inside her.

It was several moments before their breathing slowed and she fell against him, her breasts soft and warm against his chest. He started kneading her back, his hands cupping her bottom and then going back up to her shoulders and back down again. She sighed against his neck, her hot breath making his body begin to stir once more while they were still joined together.

"I could make love to you all night and day," he said. She was so amazing. This was all so amazing.

She murmured something against his chest and he stopped kneading so he could raise her head.

"What did you say, Kyla?"

"I said, *I'm game if you are*," she told him with a shy smile.

That was all it took to waken him right back up. Keeping their bodies still fused, Tanner somehow flipped her over onto her back without letting their bodies disconnect, and after kissing her properly, he did his best to make love until the morning light.

They fell asleep when the candles burned out and they were both too exhausted to go on for a single minute more.

CHAPTER NINETEEN

KYLA WOKE UP, her limbs still entangled with Tanner's and she looked over at the clock. Crap! She was late. It was Tanner's day off from the mall, but not hers. Slowly climbing from the bed, she managed to free herself and rise without waking the man.

They'd made love twice in a row, then drifted off to sleep only to wake again and make more love. Her body was sore, but she could hardly call herself unpleased with the way she felt. When she felt a rush of heat drift over her, she broke out in a broad smile.

The power was back on. Hallelujah!

Grabbing her clothes, she threw them on and then made her way out to Tanner's living room and on to the front door. She cracked it open, praying no one was there to see her do her walk of shame.

No, she wasn't ashamed they'd made love. They were

both consenting adults, but he was the first man she'd ever slept with without being in a relationship. That made her feel slightly uneasy.

But it had been great, and she refused to regret it, but she also didn't want him to think that she would now have all of these expectations of him. How could she? She didn't know a heck of a lot about the guy. As a matter of fact, she didn't even know Tanner's last name.

As she snuck into her apartment, that thought hit her full force. She'd just spent the night in bed with a man whose last name she didn't know. What did that make her?

No. She wasn't going to do this to herself. She couldn't take it back, and even if she could, she didn't want to. It had been nearly three years since she'd made love to a man, years since she'd allowed herself a night of pleasure, passion with no guilt, no shame. She wasn't going to take that away from herself.

After a quick shower, Kyla dressed and then slipped from her apartment. She was late to work at the mall, and she really hoped she didn't lose her job over it. Yes, this was just a temporary job, but the agency she worked for had a lot of temp jobs, and she wanted this to lead to another one. She couldn't blow her chances, even as an elf. She didn't get very many hours with her other position as a part-time waitress.

"Hello, Kyla. Is everything okay?"

Kyla stopped as she ran into Wayne, the security guard who gave her the creeps. She hated feeling that way about anyone at all, especially someone who was there to protect

them here, but she just didn't like the guy and she wanted
to be as far from him as possible.

"Everything is fine," she said uneasily. "I'm just running
late for work." She began moving forward again toward the
front door of the building.

"You weren't too frightened last night, were you, with the
power outage?"

"Yes. To be honest, it did frighten me, but the power is
back on, so there's no more problem." She gave a nervous
laugh.

"I checked in on you, but you weren't in your apartment
last night."

The way he said this sent chills down her spine. The
sooner she could get out of here, the better. "That was very
kind of you, Wayne, but there are people here who need to
be checked on a lot more than I do."

"I like checking on you. Did I see you in the video feed
that you went down to the basement?"

That stopped her in her tracks again, and a shudder
passed through her. "Yes. I was trying to see if the breaker
could be switched, but it was in bad shape. It seems they
must have fixed it sometime between when I was down there
and when I got back up."

"You really shouldn't go down there, not without a guard,
at least. You never know what you'll find or what can happen.
Was someone with you? It was dark, and it was hard to put
a face to the people in that feed."

"I wasn't alone, and I agree, that basement isn't a place for anyone to be going down into in the middle of the night. I am running really late, though, so I need to leave," she said, taking another step away.

"Of course. I don't want to make you late." But he grabbed her arm and stopped her. No, she wouldn't say he did it in a threatening way, but it still made an unpleasant shiver travel down her back. "I wanted to ask if you would like to go out sometime?"

His words stopped her in her tracks. That was the last thing she'd been expecting from him. Wasn't it inappropriate to be asking out someone in the building he was guarding? She didn't want to upset him, but she certainly didn't want to go on a date with the fellow.

"I'm…um…actually seeing someone right now," she said. She wasn't, really — yes, she'd just slept with Tanner, but they weren't an item, and she hadn't the least idea whether they would sleep together again, but he was a convenient excuse to get out of what she knew would be an awkward date. "I really do have to go," she told the guard as firmly as she could, and then she pulled her arm from his grip, pushed through the doors, and practically ran from the building, her horror story fully in her mind again. She couldn't even imagine being down in that dark basement with Wayne. Just the thought of it sent a whole new level of terror racing through her body.

She knew the man was most likely harmless, but with the power outages, and her imagination, and her aversion to this particular man, her mind was running a million different scenarios through her mind.

Kyla made it to the mall, and luckily she wasn't too late. No one reamed her out or threatened to call her employer, so she spent the day trying to make children happy. But her mind couldn't help but wander. What had she gotten herself into? It seemed her life was one big roller coaster and she wasn't sure when she was going to be flipped upside down again.

After her shift she would have to visit with Billy's grandmother. She really hoped the woman woke up soon. The boy had dealt with enough loss to last him a lifetime, and he certainly didn't need to lose his grandmother on top of losing his parents.

Her paperwork was filled out, and she would be there for the child if she could. Maybe they needed each other.

Her night of pleasure was certainly over — that was all she could say. The real world was intruding with a big splash, and she didn't like it one little bit.

CHAPTER TWENTY

I WANT ALL the information you can find about Billy Stephens and his grandmother, Vivian Stephens." Tanner waited for his assistant's answer before he added, "No one is to know about this."

Without another word, he hung up. Why he even cared about this pathetic little kid was beyond him, but he'd been restless all day, pacing in his apartment, and he needed something to occupy his mind. How the hell had Kyla had been able to sneak away from his bed without his knowing it?

He didn't normally fall asleep with a woman still in his bed, but the only reason he'd let Kyla stay in bed with him was to help maintain body heat and because she'd told him she was frightened of the dark. Yeah, that's all it was. But even while nodding his head in agreement with what he was saying to himself, for heaven's sake, he had to admit she was different.

He could tell himself all he wanted that he was going to walk away from her and never look back, but this small woman, this woman who was completely unsuited for him, was quickly wedging herself into his life.

He didn't like that. Didn't like it one little bit. And he would fight it like hell.

He'd just have to fight it until Christmas day, when he'd run like hell back to his bachelor heaven high in the Seattle sky. Take things one day at a time — wasn't that what you had to do? Accept the things you couldn't change? Suck it up? But a few more little fixes wouldn't hurt. One thing Tanner knew for sure was that he wanted her back in his bed again tonight.

Waiting for her to arrive back home after work was killing him. Yes, he'd called the authorities and asked permission to walk over to the mall to accompany her here, and they'd denied him. They'd already let him go to the hospital, had let him have some leniency, they'd pointed out.

This damn ankle device was pissing him off. "Only a few more days to go," he reminded himself out loud.

He was a good man, a man who gave to the community, who provided jobs, who obeyed the law. The two officers who'd so gleefully escorted him to this effing building didn't seem to feel the same way, though. Well, to hell with them. He was only here for a little longer.

Okay, he had to admit that the thought of leaving and never seeing Kyla again was far less than appealing. But who knew what would happen in the next few days? He would just cling to the happy thought that he was temporarily insane, most likely from the mold he knew had to be everywhere in this old building.

When Kyla didn't arrive back at the complex soon after her shift was over, he began to worry. What if something had happened to her? When two hours passed, he was about to break the law and go looking for her.

After a few more minutes, he made his way purposefully to the front doors of the building, not caring if the damn officers came and arrested him. She could be in trouble, and he needed to make sure she was okay.

Just as he pushed the doors open, she came through. He gave her no greeting as she looked up, startled, then quickly looked back down again. This wasn't good. She wouldn't even look him in the eyes.

"Where were you?" The question wasn't meant to come out as so curt, but he'd been worried, dammit.

"What business is it of yours, Tanner?" she said as she looked back up, fire instantly leaping in her eyes.

"I was worried." Again, Tanner was shocked when those were the words that popped from his mouth. He didn't worry about people, and if he did, he certainly didn't admit it.

"Oh." Her temper quickly defused. "I went to visit Vivian. She still isn't awake, but she looks better. The doctor said he expects her to wake up any time."

"That's wonderful." Should he admit that he was checking on Billy, that he was trying to see if there was anything he could do for the boy? No. He shouldn't, not yet, at least. He'd hold that card to his chest and bring it out when it would play to his best advantage. If he helped the kid — an act of boredom, of course — wouldn't that make him more appealing to Kyla? Weren't girls a sucker for a man coming to the rescue? Yes, they were. He was only helping the kid to get back into her pants. That thought made him feel better, and he refused to even think to himself that he was lying, even in his own head.

"I tried to get information on Billy, but they won't tell me anything. Did you know the process to become a foster parent is long and drawn out? By the time I could do anything, his grandmother will be fully recovered. I've still started the paperwork. I just hate the thought of him being all alone and scared."

"I know you hated handing him over, but if you hadn't done that, you would have been considered a kidnapper. You did the right thing, Kyla."

"It doesn't matter if I did the right thing or not. I feel like I've betrayed him, and he's already been through so much. It's just…it's not right," she said, her shoulders sagging.

"Why don't you come over? I'll make you some dinner and we can talk about it…" Nice offer, he thought.

"I can't tonight, Tanner. I'm so tired. I want a hot bath and to go to sleep. It's pathetic, but it is what it is. And I am what I am."

Before he was able to argue with her, or maybe persuade her, she turned and walked way from him. He was so surprised that he'd been rejected, and by a woman who knew all his best bedroom tricks — okay, not all of them — that by the time he realized she was getting away, she was already at her apartment and her door was shutting. Maybe he'd just go pound on it.

"Ouch. That looked like it hurt."

Tanner turned around, fury rolling through him.

"Who in the hell are you?"

"Hey, don't take your bad mood out on me. I'm Wayne, one of the guards here."

"Well, I'd appreciate it if you keep your comments to yourself," Tanner told him as he turned to leave.

"I'm just saying that she's not the warmest cookie in the batch. The lady up on three-twelve heats up a whole lot faster," Wayne said with a sly look.

"Go to hell," Tanner said, and he slammed his door in the guard's face.

It looked as if Wayne wouldn't have a job come morning.

Tanner flopped down on the couch and made two more phone calls. This insane restlessness really pissed him off. He didn't need Kyla to be with him to make him happy. It had to be this place. As soon as he got out of here, he would go back to being himself.

And that's just what he wanted.

CHAPTER TWENTY-ONE

" ...AND A BUZZ Lightyear, and Megatron, and..."
The kid wanted a million presents for Christmas, and
Tanner tuned him out. He didn't care. If anything,
this job had shown him that the majority of people were
just plain greedy.

Not one child had touched him like Billy had almost
three weeks before. He'd gotten the information back that
he'd requested, but he almost wished he could erase from
his mind what the report said.

Billy's father had been a soldier, had been deployed for
a year, and he'd just gotten home for leave. His wife, Billy's
mother, had picked him up from the airport and they'd gone
over a bridge. Billy hadn't even gotten to see his father again.

One minute he was asleep in bed with no idea that his
father was coming home, and the next he'd been awakened
to see his grandmother's sad face, and to hear her telling him

he was going to come live with her now.

The two of them had a lot of healing to do, and now Billy blamed himself for his grandmother getting hurt. She was awake, but it would have almost been better if she hadn't come out of the coma.

When the doctors had gone in to fix the hip, they'd found bone cancer. It was too far gone for them — or anyone — to do anything about it. So Billy was not only not going to not get his Christmas wish of having his parents come home again, but he was going to lose his only other living relative.

Tanner was trying desperately not to dwell on it, but as he looked out at the line of kids still waiting to sit on his lap, have a picture taken and tell him how many toys they wanted, all he could think about was one small boy. But he did his best to shake Billy's image from his mind. The boy wasn't his responsibility. Kyla wasn't either. He was almost done with this place, and once his stint was over, he was done forever, so how could these two people occupy so much of his time?

Shaking his head, he practically pushed away the little boy who was actually on his lap. Still, he wasn't wholly in Scrooge mode. A semblance of a smile touched his lips as a little blond girl with big brown eyes and rosy cheeks took the boy's place on Tanner's lap.

"What can Santa bring you for Christmas?" he asked.

She flashed him a precious little grin. "I want a purple pony," she giggled.

"A purple pony?" Did they even make things like that?

"Yes, Santa, with sparkles."

"Santa will have to talk to his elves and see if we can get you one of those," he told her. At least she wasn't reading off a list from a yard-long scroll. The twinkle in her eyes was just plain adorable.

"Thanks, Santa. I love you," the little girl said.

"Santa loves you too," he told her, and accepted her hug. All right, this wasn't so bad. He was just feeling grumpy about humanity earlier.

Then she leaned back and the color washed from her face. "Uh oh." That was his only warning before her mouth opened and a stream of nastiness came shooting out right at him. He'd gone from a generic horror movie to The Exorcist.

Tanner froze as the smell of vomit invaded his nostrils and chunks of food got stuck in his fake beard. His so-called helpers all took a few steps back; the best they could do for him, it seemed, was give him wide-eyed looks of horror.

"Sorry, Santa," the little girl said before she quickly climbed off his lap and ran to her mother, tears now pouring from her eyes.

"It's okay, sweetie. You didn't mean to throw up on Santa," her mother told her.

"Now he won't bring me my pony," she sobbed.

"Of course that's why she's crying," Tanner muttered. "Greedy like every damn one of them. I'm done for the day! Now!"

With that, he stood up and stomped from the ridiculously festive "North Pole" area, walking through the mall with people skirting around him, his stink following wherever he went. He'd been peed on, spit on, punched, snotted on, and now thrown up on. How in the hell did they get anyone to actually take this job? There was no amount of money in the universe that would make being Santa worth it.

All children were simply germ machines out to wreck the lives of unsuspecting adults. Who in their right mind would actually want to have some of the repulsive little brats for their own? And Billy? He was probably a little schemer, too, playing his bereavement for all it was worth.

Tanner entered the break room, and he found Kyla sitting on the bench and rubbing her feet.

"Why in the hell weren't you out there?"

Her shocked look made him realize that, in his anger, he might be behaving slightly over the top. But he was covered in vomit. Didn't that give him a little bit of leeway to act out?

"I'm on break," she said before her nose twitched and then she backed away from him. "What on earth happened?"

"What do you think happened? Anything and everything disgusting a child can do to me has now been done. Thank heavens I only have one more day left of this Santa bullshit!"

"It's not so bad. They're just children, and they adore you," she reminded him.

"Just children? How can you even say that? You've seen their behavior. They are all monsters in disguise. Don't let their small size fool you," he ranted as he stripped down.

When his eyes connected with hers again and he saw the look of appreciation that his naked torso inspired in her face, his temper cooled. No, they hadn't made love again in the last two days, and yes, she'd managed to avoid him like he had the plague, but she still wanted him. That much was obvious.

There were only two nights left in his sentence, and he planned on making the most of the time. "How about we sneak out of here? I no longer have a usable Santa suit, so they're going to have to bring in the other guy. We can go cuddle up and watch another Christmas movie."

The last thing he wanted to do was watch a movie, but if that got her to snuggle into him, then he would watch a dozen of the things. Their first movie night hadn't been half bad — well, it hadn't until she'd fallen asleep. And he did have to sit through Jimmy Stewart and Donna Reed.

"I can't just leave work, Tanner," she said, looking down.

"Why are you avoiding me? Do you regret what happened between us?" There. She couldn't get out of answering that.

"No. I decided not to regret it, but it doesn't mean that it's going to happen again," she said, looking back up with a glint of determination in her eyes.

"Why not? We're good together. Why fight it?" Logic was always the answer, wasn't it?

"Just because we're obviously compatible in bed doesn't mean we should continue to jump into it."

"In my book, that's exactly what it means." Women! Were they all incapable of reason?

"Look, it's obvious you're not sticking around long, Tanner, and I'm not usually a one-night-stand sort of girl, so let's not have regrets, but let's not pretend there's something there between us."

He latched on to the one part of her explanation he could. "It won't be a one-night stand if we do it again."

"Are you for real?" she asked, a hint of a smile on her face.

"Oh, baby, I'm all real," he assured her as he stepped closer.

Her nose wrinkled for the second time, and she stood up and backed away. "Why don't you go and shower? Your looks might be appealing, but your smell is killing the mood."

With that lethal shot, she walked out of the room. He almost followed before he realized he was standing there in his boxers and ridiculously thick socks. With a sigh, he grabbed his clothes and made his way to the mall shower.

The sad thing about the shower was that it was better than the one in his apartment. But that was hardly an issue anymore.

Kyla was the issue. She might think she was avoiding him successfully, and she might think she was witty, but she didn't know quite how determined he could be.

She was soon to find out.

CHAPTER TWENTY-TWO

ONLY A DAY to go in his previously rodent-infested, leaky-piped, ball-freezing building. OK, the temperature was still miserable in here, but everything else was so wretched, the temperature might as well follow suit.

Tanner had to smile when he found himself humming Christmas carols. He was done for the day — the mall closed early on Christmas Eve so the employees could celebrate with their families — and he'd donned a Santa suit for the last time. With something approaching glee, he tossed the stupid suit into the costume return, giving it an extra little shove just to say *good riddance*, and he walked away from the mall with a smile.

Kyla hadn't been working there that day. Lucky girl. She was at her other job, which had to be better than dealing with snot-nosed kids, whatever it was. But he wasn't so lucky, because her absence had made the time drag by for him. The uncertainty and anticipation didn't help. It was his last night with her and he wanted to make it count. She hadn't said what her plans for the evening were, but since she didn't have any family left, he was hoping they could spend it together. He'd ordered a nice catered dinner, which would arrive in a couple of hours.

The two of them could eat an exquisite meal and then cuddle up on the couch. The night before, she'd rejected his offer of watching another cheesy Christmas flick, but she couldn't do that now, could she? Not on Christmas Eve. And this time she wouldn't fall asleep, because he'd be treating her to all of his best moves. And he already knew how much she liked them.

It was time they got reacquainted. Since they'd made love nearly a week ago, the sexual tension had been building to the boiling point — at least for him — and he was more than ready to refuel the magic the two of them made together. It was tonight or never, because once he left this building, he wouldn't be back.

As usual, that thought sent an odd pang through him, but he chose to ignore it. Sure, he'd been getting a bit sappy about this particular woman, but people in extreme circumstances tended to act against their character. He'd heard about that in the movie *Speed*.

This wasn't his life. He was happy with who he was outside of this alternate reality, living in his penthouse apartment, working day and night, and sporting a tuxedo when he consumed champagne and caviar instead of beer and hot wings.

This existence was beneath him. He didn't consider himself a snob; he was just a man who had worked hard and liked the finer things in life. There was nothing wrong with that. Okay, he conceded, he did have a wealthy family, and he did seem to have the Midas touch.

When he reached the apartment building, Tanner's imagination was running along so vividly that he could practically taste Kyla's skin on his lips. And as he turned the corner to their end of the hallway, he wasn't paying attention and ran smack dab into her, nearly making her fall back on her tush.

She was in an awful hurry.

"Oh, sorry," she gasped before looking up and discovering who it was. "Hey, Tanner. Sorry, I don't have time to chat. I'm running late," she said as she attempted to get past him.

"Where are you going?" he asked, resolutely blocking her path.

"I have plans tonight."

Vague, to say the least, and he wasn't about to let her get away with it. "What plans?" he asked suspiciously. This was supposed to be their night together. She couldn't possibly be seeing another man. He would know. Wouldn't he? Maybe not. She'd been able to avoid him way too often for his liking.

"I just have plans." She looked down, refusing to meet his gaze.

Instant jealousy slammed into his gut. Maybe she *was*

seeing another man.

"I thought we'd have dinner together tonight. I ordered it in."

Her eyebrows rose. "You ordered Christmas dinner? Doesn't a holiday meal mean that you're supposed to slave over a hot stove all day?"

"I don't cook elaborate meals, just breakfast, and preferably after a night of working up a good appetite," he said as he tried to turn her around.

"Yeah, my dad 'helped' my mom once or twice in the kitchen for elaborate dinners," Kyla said, "but it was an utter disaster. Whenever he tried to again, she would end up chasing him away, telling him he would mess everything up." A melancholy smile rose up on her lips.

"Besides, isn't it better to have a nice meal without being exhausted from cooking all day and night?" he asked, trying to tempt her into changing her mind.

"No, Tanner. Part of the appeal of a great Christmas dinner is in knowing that it was prepared with love." Even the little smile she'd had not so long before disappeared when she said those words.

This wasn't good. He wanted her happy and carefree tonight, not sinking back into a happy past that she could never have again.

"I'll have to remember that," he said, but he wouldn't — at least if he avoided family at big holidays as often as he did. Would he remember her? After tonight, they wouldn't see each other again.

"I really do have to go. I'm very late." She tried to get around him for the second time.

"Seriously, where?"

If she wasn't going to stay in with him, then he damn well wanted to know where she was in such a rush to go.

She hesitated, then sighed. "I'm serving dinner tonight at a homeless shelter nearby."

Whew. It wasn't a date with someone else, after all. A date on Christmas Eve probably meant the relationship had to be going somewhere — like church.

"Why?" he asked before he was able to stop himself.

"Because I don't have a family to celebrate with anymore, and I figure I can give something back. I know it's what my mom would do if she were still here and all alone."

"I'll come with you." Oh, no. What had he just said? The last thing Tanner wanted to do was hang out in some crappy kitchen and serve food to people who lived on the streets. Why were they homeless, anyway? It didn't make sense to him why anyone would choose that kind of life. They were clearly too lazy to work.

"Um…you don't need to do that," she said, looking at him coolly.

Was his disdain so obvious?

"I want to." He told himself it was just because he wanted to get her alone later. Surely, if he were to come with her to serve food to these homeless people, she would thaw enough that he'd finally get her into Santa's sack again.

"I don't know, Tanner. I don't think it's really your kind

of place."

Her lack of faith in him rankled. Granted, he was thinking the same thing, but to have those words come from her mouth didn't make him happy at all.

"Let me just go and make a phone call. Promise not to leave without me," he said, giving her his sternest look.

"I guess," she replied, and she leaned against the wall. She didn't look at all convinced that he'd come back from his apartment.

Tanner rushed inside and pulled out the card for the police station monitoring his ridiculous ankle device. Damn! He hated that he had to ask for permission to go anywhere. One more day, he told himself. He only had one more day. Actually, less than that!

His call was picked up on the third ring, and though the officer, who just happened to be the one who'd dropped him off on that first day, gave him permission to serve a meal at the homeless shelter, the guy actually had the audacity to laugh and tell Tanner, "*Good luck!*"

Still, Tanner probably needed all the luck he could get.

His second call was to his assistant. Het told Randy to have the meal set up and ready for when they returned. They might be starting later than Tanner wanted, but he was still going to follow through on his plans of seducing his little Christmas elf. That one night wasn't anywhere near enough.

When he walked back out into the hallway, he was relieved to see her still there. She was looking at her watch with a frown on her face, but she'd waited for him.

"All set," he said, with the best smile he knew how to fake. He took her arm, placing it through his. "How far away is this place?"

"It's only about a mile, but we're running really late, so we'd better get a cab," she told him.

It took only a couple of minutes before a taxi drove by, and Tanner flagged it down with no problem. The cab driver talked nonstop, and Tanner had to fight his irritation when Kyla leaned over the seat and started to converse with the guy. She even sounded excited. Of course, Tanner had nothing to be jealous about, so why did it bother him to share her attention? Ridiculous.

When they got to the shelter, it took everything in him not to wrinkle his nose at the crowd before him. There was a group of men outside, some in threadbare clothing; had those guys bathed in a month? The pungent smell of urine and body odor wafted in his direction. How was he going to get through the night?

"This way," Kyla told him and led him down a small alley and inside through a side door. It took all his willpower not to turn and make sure someone wasn't coming up behind him to pick his pocket or rob them outright.

"Kyla! I'm so glad you made it," a harried woman said. "I was beginning to worry. The twins both got food poisoning and we're a couple of people short." She tossed an apron at Kyla before noticing Tanner. It was almost comical the way the woman's eyes widened.

"Hi, Maggie," Kyla said. "This is Tanner, my neighbor.

He wanted to help tonight. Maybe since he's the size of the twins put together, he can make up for their absence." With a laugh, she went over to the sink and began scrubbing up.

"Well, I won't complain about an extra set of hands." Maggie walked to a small desk, grabbed another apron, and tossed it to Tanner.

He took off his coat, slipped the apron on, and washed his hands at the sink Kyla had just finished using.

Maggie got into work mode, directing the two of them to where she wanted them, and the next couple of hours passed by in a blur as Tanner stood at a long table in between Kyla and a girl who couldn't have been more than sixteen, and they proceeded to dish up dinner to a seemingly never-ending line of people.

"Bless you."

Tanner woke up from his daze to find in front of him a petite, dark-haired woman with a small child clinging to her leg. What in the world was a woman like her doing homeless — and with such a young boy? He wanted to ask, but he held his tongue.

"Merry Christmas," he replied instead, surprised by the number of people he'd served who didn't seem at all the type he would classify as homeless.

"Not everything is as it appears," the woman said, as if reading his mind.

"I'm not judging," he said quickly, feeling like an ass, knowing full well that's what he'd been doing.

"You are, but that's all right. I used to be exactly the same way while I worked for a prestigious law firm. My husband died and then my boss decided that since I was single, I must be a merry widow and I'd make a great plaything. When I didn't give him what he wanted, he fired me. I tried filing a sexual-harassment suit, but they didn't become the top lawyers in the area because they were stupid. I soon found that not only was I out of a job, but I also couldn't get another one anywhere else — my former boss had been smearing my name. Nice guy. Anyway, just because people find themselves running out of options doesn't mean they chose that life for themself."

Weird. She sounded strong but still defeated. At the same time.

The boy tucked in at her side couldn't have been more than three or four. He was wearing warm clothes and good shoes. It was obvious that all she had went into caring for the young lad.

"I'm sorry," Tanner said. He hoped he didn't look as foolish as he felt.

"I'm used to it now. All of that began a year ago. We recently ran out of money and lost the house. My husband was a good man, but he didn't make a lot of money and our savings were small. I tried to make what we had last, but it could only go so far. I won't stay down for long, though. I have my son to worry about."

Before Tanner could say anything more, she moved on, and the line continued. When the last of the people got their plates, Tanner found himself gazing at the empty trays and the smiling faces of the patrons.

Though some were obviously disheartened to be in this situation, they were still grateful to be in a warm room with a bunch of people who, for this night at least, were their family. Even though they were strangers.

Tanner found it humbling.

Kyla went out among the people, taking them extra biscuits and filling their glasses with water. Other workers were passing out candy to the children and small items such as new toothbrushes and toothpaste.

The people's eyes lit up as if they were receiving priceless gifts. How long had Tanner taken everything he had for granted? He'd grown up wealthy, never having a thing to worry about. He knew that he'd always get his next meal, that there would always be a warm bed for him to crawl into. His life had been easy.

Well, it had been tough since the beginning of the month. And what if it became like one of those lives he was seeing now, and for the long term — what if his luck suddenly ran out, and fate just kept throwing him curve ball after curve ball? He'd been thrown a few in his life, but never to this extent, never to the point that he had to worry about keeping a roof over his head or food in his stomach.

Wandering around the tables set up for people he was only beginning to understand, he didn't take long to find the woman and her small child. She was smiling as she unwrapped a chocolate bar for her son and handed it to him. The boy took a bite and grinned so sweetly that it took

Tanner a moment to clear the lump in his throat.

"What's your name?" he asked when he could finally speak. Then he sat next to her.

"Morgan," she said somewhat warily.

"What did you do for the law firm, Morgan?"

She looked in his eyes, as if assessing his motives for asking. Tanner wondered how many people had tried to take advantage of her since she'd been on her own. He probably didn't want to know.

"I'm a paralegal, so just about everything. I miss the hustle and bustle of the business world, but I try to look at the positives. I have so much one-on-one time with my son, after all, even if it has to be done in a shelter."

Tanner recognized that gleam in her eyes, that desire to be at the top of your game. Without any hesitation, he reached into his pocket, pulled out his wallet, and retrieved a business card.

"My name is Tanner Storm and my father has a company in downtown Seattle. Tell him that I sent you and want you to come in for a job interview on Monday. No, in case you're worried, there are no strings attached to this offer."

"Why would you do this?" Morgan asked, her expression changing to complete shock and her voice choking up. Her hand shook slightly as she took the card he'd just written his father's number on.

"Because I don't intimidate easily and I think what your former bosses did to you is horrific. If you want a good job, I'll help you get your foot in the door. The rest will be up to you." He rose to leave her and her son to their holiday.

Her hand shot out and she gripped his arm. She was silent for a minute while she tried to pull herself together. Tanner waited, unaware that Kyla was watching the exchange from across the room, though she couldn't hear what was being said.

"Merry Christmas, Mr. Storm," Morgan told him. "Thank you for this. You have given me and my son the best gift anyone has ever given us. Even if I'm not hired, your kindness has touched me deeply. You're a good man," she said as a tear escaped.

Her last sentence rang in his head. Was he a good man?

"Morgan, I can't begin to tell you what *you* have given me tonight," he said through strained vocal cords. He put his hand over hers and nodded to underline his sincerity.

He turned and walked away, a heaviness in his chest. How wrong he'd been about people. He'd always just assumed that those who were homeless were there of their own free will. He'd never taken the time to understand that maybe, just maybe, they hadn't chosen their circumstances.

"What was that all about?"

Tanner turned to find Kyla looking at him suspiciously.

"Merry Christmas, Kyla."

Looking up, he noticed the mistletoe right above their heads. He hauled her against him without any delay and kissed her, a sweet and relatively short kiss that still showed her how much he needed her. When he released her, the two of them heard a few chuckles, and several people clapped, but his eyes were for her only.

"Let's go home," he said, and the look he gave her left no doubt of his meaning.

"I would like that," she murmured.

For a moment, Tanner thought he'd misunderstood, but as her hand slipped into his, he knew what she was agreeing to. His heart kicking into high gear, he led her through the dining room and to the kitchen, where he grabbed their coats and then quickly led her outside.

He needed to get her back to the apartment building before she changed her mind. This was looking to be the merriest Christmas he'd ever had, broken pipes, Santa suit and all.

CHAPTER TWENTY-THREE

K YLA HELD TIGHTLY to Tanner's hand. She was
a nervous wreck now. Was this a wise path for her
to be going down? Should she climb back into this
bed? The clock was counting down on their time. No, he
hadn't told her he was leaving, but she knew he was. Tanner
was not a man who lived in the trenches.

She'd told herself she wouldn't regret their night together,
and she didn't. It had been too wonderful for her ever to
have regrets. However, she'd also told herself she wouldn't
join him in his bed again. To do so, she feared, would lock
her to him emotionally in a way that she couldn't reverse.

But Tanner had been so kind to the people at the shelter
and to her earlier this evening; it was like seeing a different
man, and it had made her heart swell, knocked down the
last of her defenses. Was it because it was Christmas Eve
and she was tired of being left with nothing but ghosts and

memories? Had her thoughts about how alone in the world she was ramped up her vulnerability to an all-time high? Whatever the reason, she didn't want to change her mind.

As she and Tanner sped down the hall of their apartment building, her nerves were shot, yes, but her heart was thundering. She wanted this, wanted it desperately. And there was no doubt that Tanner wanted it even more. He unlocked his apartment door and opened it wide for her to step through. When he shut it again and put his hands on her shoulders, she jumped and then laughed as he removed her jacket and hung it on the hook by the door. Not one word had been said since she'd agreed to come back to his apartment, agreed to make love to him again.

"Sorry. I guess I'm a bit tense." She looked up and boldly met his gaze, though every instinct in her made her want to look away and hide from what she was feeling.

"I'm not going to attack…though I want to," he said. "And I'm good at handling tension."

Somehow the need she heard in his voice calmed her. Her muscles relaxed and she even managed to smile. They were both consenting adults, and they'd already done this once, proved they were more than suited to climb into bed together. She had nothing to be nervous about, nothing to fear — well, except for the utter loneliness she was sure to feel after being with a man like Tanner and then being alone all over again when he inevitably disappeared.

The smell of food filled her nose, distracting her from her morose thoughts and making her stomach rumble.

Though she'd spent a few hours serving dinner, she'd been too busy all night to eat so much as a single morsel of bread, and she realized that she was famished. She turned around to see Tanner's table covered with a lovely and festive red tablecloth, and expertly set with gleaming china and silver.

"When did you have time to do this?" she asked. Going in closer, she found a wonderful Christmas dinner with all the trimmings sitting on top of warmers on the kitchen counter.

"Why not think of this as a sort of holiday magic? Maybe I really *am* Santa Claus." Tanner smiled and held out a chair.

Maybe he was. She hadn't cried this holiday season, and she'd decorated a tree, and made gingerbread cookies. Had Tanner come into her life to help heal her? She didn't know the answers and she wasn't sure she needed to know. One thing that she had no doubt about was that there was far more to Tanner than initially met the eye.

"You're not the type of guy who ever would normally live in a place like this." It wasn't a question, and she was afraid of what he would say next, but why should she? She'd known almost since the beginning that Tanner didn't fit in here. This wasn't some great revelation.

He paused and looked at her almost guiltily — but that made no sense. What could he possibly feel guilty for? That he was slumming it? That he was playing games with the down-on-her-luck girl?

"I just want a piece of mystery between us," he told her. "We're two strangers who happened to fall into each other's path, and tonight is all about how we make each other feel, not about who we are. I think you realize that we don't have a future together. I don't want to lie to you about that. But we're two people who need each other now — tonight. We should take wonder where we find it."

Two lost souls on the highway of life? She knew she should try to learn something real, something legitimate about this man before giving him her body for a second time, but she couldn't seem to look away, couldn't seem to break the spell that he'd woven around her. Should she keep fighting this? Which would bring her more regrets than she already had — if she walked away right now, or if she stayed? Ugh! She just didn't know.

What she did know, though, was that even if she did end up regretting anything she'd done, she'd also have the good memories to counteract the bad ones from that horrific Christmastime two years before. They'd made love once, and it had been magnificent. Yes, her time with Tanner was coming to a close. She felt that in the air, knew he would soon be gone — he'd said so openly from the first moment sparks had flown between them. Like any good magical being, he'd be off in a poof of smoke.

Silence stretched on between them, but it wasn't awkward, wasn't unbearable. Tanner poured her a glass of wine, and she looked into his mesmerizing eyes before allowing a nervous giggle to escape.

"Wow, if you knew the thoughts running through my mind, you might try to run as fast as you can," she said when he raised an eyebrow at her little burst of laughter.

She sipped her wine and prayed that her nerves would calm down.

"I don't think a bulldozer crashing through the walls of this building could make me run from you," he said, his eyes boring into her.

"If the owner of this building gets his way, Tanner, a bulldozer putting a damper on the mood could just happen."

He flinched and turned away, but she didn't take any offense. She was actually relieved to be released from the intense look in his eyes.

"Sometimes things happen for a reason, Kyla. Maybe you were meant to be in these apartments to take the next step in your life," he said, and she couldn't disagree with that. "And maybe by being forced to leave, it will help you take another step in your life." This last part seemed to be spoken in an almost desperate way.

"Is that what you want, Tanner? Do you want someone else to force you to make a decision?"

His body tensed and her eyes were locked on his back as she waited for him to turn back around. Talk about dampers. This conversation was doing a real number on them and their mood, killing the eagerness they'd felt earlier to get back here and tear each other's clothes off. But at the same time, it was actually making it easier for her to fall back into his bed. She felt she was getting to know him just a tiny bit.

"I've always made my own decisions," he said before letting out a sigh and turning back toward her. "I didn't choose to be here, but I'm grateful for this moment, grateful to be standing in this exact place with you right in front of me. Sometimes we're pushed to do something we normally would never do, and we might fight it, and we might look back and still be angry about it, but there's a reason for everything, and I have no doubt that I was meant to be here with you right here and right now. 'To everything, turn, turn, turn...'"

He stepped toward her and cupped her cheek, and Kyla found herself on the verge of tears.

"So we quit fighting this, right?" she said, nuzzling against his hand.

"We quit fighting what has been inevitable from the moment I laid eyes on you, from the first moment our lips connected, from the magical instant our bodies became one. We don't worry about tomorrow; we only appreciate what we have right now."

"Do you practice these lines, Tanner?" She was desperately trying to break the intensity of the moment.

"I've never said anything like this to another woman. Ever. I don't lie, and I won't make promises that I can't or won't keep, but when I look at you, I can't look away. When I'm away from you, I want to rush to your arms. You have been messing with my head from the very first moment you stole into my apartment."

"Well, then, Tanner, I'm glad to be guilty of my one and only instance of breaking and entering."

"I'm glad, too." He leaned forward and captured her lips in a sweet kiss that had her head spinning. Who needed wine?

But just when she was ready to grab hold of him, he let her go, kissing her quickly one more time before moving away. "I need to feed you," he said. She leaned back while she watched him fill her plate.

The atmosphere, the food, the wine. And the perfection of it all. More than anything else in the past two years, it made her miss her parents. Each and every holiday, her mother would be in charge of a beautiful production, laying the table with their finest china, crafting desserts for days and putting together the best dinner a person could manage.

Not much that Tanner was serving looked like her mother's dishes — Kyla didn't recognize some of the food at all — but the setting, the holiday decorations on the table, all of it…it made her miss "home." Maybe it was time to go back there, to walk through the halls and see what she'd cut herself off from two years ago. Instead of confronting this constant emptiness, maybe she would feel as if her family were with her.

"After you." Tanner pulled her from her thoughts once again when he set her plate down and held her chair out for her.

"Thank you."

Dinner proceeded quietly as Kyla tried to push out thoughts of her lost family from her mind. She was with a striking man who had gone all out to give her a beautiful holiday. She was determined to enjoy this moment to its fullest.

Needing the ache to go away, she set down her fork, two glasses of wine giving her the extra boost of courage she desperately needed. Rising with purpose, she moved slowly around the table to where Tanner was sitting. With a smile, he pushed back his chair and waited for her to make the next move. Straddling his legs, she sat down on his lap and wrapped her arms around his neck.

"Make love to me," she whispered, and she connected their mouths.

Tanner hesitated no longer. He returned her embrace, deepened the kiss, and, as he let his hands travel beneath her sweater, scorched her skin with his touch.

"Yes, Tanner," she moaned as he cupped her breasts, sending flames shooting straight to her core. This was the magic only he seemed able to bring, and she was a fool to even think one time in his arms had been enough. Why fight the inevitable? Why fight what her body needed? There was no reason, and she was a fool for even considering it.

Tanner broke away from her, making her whimper until she realized he was holding the bottom of her sweater. With a quick motion, he tugged it over her head and threw it somewhere behind them, then pulled her back against him and let his hands roam across the skin of her back.

She felt him unclasp her bra as he continued to worship her mouth, driving her loneliness away and replacing it with excitement and pleasure. Yes, this is exactly what she needed. This was the best Christmas gift he could possibly give her. When he removed her bra and then his shirt, she delighted to feel her straining nipples rub against the smooth skin of his broad chest.

"Please, Tanner, I want more." He trailed his mouth down her throat, licking her skin, soothing one ache only to cause another.

"I'll give you everything," he promised, and moved her from his lap so they both could stand up.

Lifting her into his arms, he carried her to the kitchen, much to her surprise, and set her down in front of the counter. She looked at him with a question in her eyes, but he just smiled as he undid her jeans and peeled them from her legs, his eyes lighting up at the sight of her panties.

A full-on blush suffused her cheeks when she remembered her impulsive buy. She squirmed in front of him. Obviously, she hadn't been expecting to make love this beautiful Christmas Eve.

"I love them," he said, chortling as he began removing her Rudolph panties.

"Ummm, it was a weak moment," she said, embarrassed until he kissed her stomach right above the elastic at the top of said panties. Then, he began blazing a trail of wet kisses upward to her swollen breasts.

Crying out when he clasped a nipple between his teeth, she forgot all about the poor red-nosed reindeer. When he lifted her up onto the counter, sending a few dishes crashing to the floor, she wrapped her legs around him, pulling him close.

Once again joining his lips to hers, he quickly removed

his slacks and then pressed his body fully against hers. She reveled in the feel of his hardness.

"Yes, *please*," she told him.

She heard the ripping of foil and then he was pulling back just a bit, making her cry out in protest until she felt him come close again, and then finally he was pushing inside her.

"Oh, *yes*." Desperate for him to drive into her, she cried out her approval as he stretched her open, inch by glorious inch.

"You feel so good," he groaned as he stalled halfway inside.

"Don't stop!" she almost wailed. She wanted motion, blessed friction, and she urged him on with her gently gyrating hips.

"Hold on," he growled, giving her body time to adjust.

But she didn't want time; she wanted him — now!

For a moment, he clenched his teeth as he looked into her eyes; then he surged forward, burying himself fully inside her heat, making her head fall back as she cried out. If he moved even a little, she knew she would climax. She'd never shattered so quickly while making love. As if he could read her body, he withdrew and drove back in, sending her spiraling over the edge, making her clench around him, forcing a groan to come ripping from his throat.

He drove slowly in and out of her, prolonging her pleasure until the last of her tremors died away. Then he grabbed her head and kissed her deeply as he began to move with long, deep strokes.

Time lost all meaning as his hands explored her body and his mouth ravished hers. The beating of her heart pulsed in time with his movements. The pressure within her began building again as he continued his lovemaking, and suddenly she felt her release first rippling through her again, then rushing headlong through her body as her pleasure spiked.

As she shook in his arms, he groaned, sinking deep inside her again, pulsing, spilling, and then becoming still. His head collapsed against her shoulder as a final shudder racked his body. She tasted the saltiness of his flesh, loved the flush that had stolen over his beautiful skin.

An eternity must have passed before he drew back and looked at her passion-spent face.

"That was unbelievable," he said as he again caressed her cheek. "I didn't think anything could be better than the first time we made love, but I was wrong."

"I never want to stop," she replied, bending forward and brushing her lips against his, needing this man over and over again.

"A lady after my own heart." He lifted her from the counter and began moving through his apartment.

"Where are we going?"

"Take a guess. We're going to continue doing it over and over and over again," he said with a wicked smile.

"Oh, I must have been a very good girl this year." She laughed in delight as he set her down on his bed and quickly climbed in after her.

"Mmm, yes, you have. You're definitely on Santa's good list."

"That's too bad. I kind of like the idea of being on the naughty list," she said, then blushed.

"This just keeps getting better and better, Ms. Ridgley," he told her after a pause.

"I can't imagine it getting any better, Mr. Mystery Man, but I'm more than willing to give it all I've got. We could at least try to stay on a roll."

They didn't have to try very hard at all.

CHAPTER TWENTY-FOUR

MERRY CHRISTMAS, MR. Storm. You're a free man."

Tanner looked down at his monitor-free ankle and sent the officer a withering look. He needed these guys to get the hell out of his apartment before Kyla woke up and found them here.

When this had all begun, he'd been planning on beating the officers out of the building as soon as the ridiculous contraption had been removed. Now, it was Christmas morning and he had a beautiful woman sound asleep in his bed.

He and Kyla hadn't gotten more than two or three hours of sleep the night before. Still, he felt more energized than he could ever remember feeling. He didn't know whether that was from a night of great lovemaking or because he was off house arrest, but the ankle device was history, and he could finally return to his beautiful penthouse.

Why wasn't he just writing her a note and thanking her for a great night, telling her that she could have whatever she wanted from his apartment and that it had been fun, but he was out of here? Sheesh, what a bunch of questions. But he'd gotten what he wanted. There was nothing else for them to say to each other. It was finished.

Of course, he'd never done that to a woman, and he didn't want to be the kind of man who did. Kyla wasn't some cheap hooker, and he wasn't a complete bastard. Or at least he hoped he wasn't.

Even just thinking about bailing out on her like that turned his stomach. When the officers left and he shut and locked the door right behind them, he found himself wandering back to his bedroom, just standing there in the doorway and watching the rise and fall of her beautifully bare chest as she breathed evenly in her sleep.

She was stunning both inside and out. It was depressing to think that he'd never really looked beyond the externals with any other woman he'd been with. He'd really only cared that they looked good on his arm and satisfied his needs in the bedroom.

Kyla had seemed like a completely new woman last night, much different than the shy woman he'd been with a week earlier. Her confidence with him and with her own body had made her bold and daring, and she'd taken his breath away more than once. She'd teased him once again about leaving his socks on, but he'd found a satisfying way of distracting her when she'd told him she was going to pull them off. The last thing he'd wanted was for her to find the monitor. But that was a nightmare in his life that was now over and done with.

As she began to stir, he left his position in the doorway and went to start a pot of coffee. When it had just brewed, she walked into the kitchen, her hair tumbled and his shirt the only thing covering her, offering him a tasty view of her honey-toned thighs.

"I hope you don't mind that I borrowed your shirt," she said, shifting nervously on her feet.

"You look far better in that shirt than I ever have," he said with a smile before he walked over and leaned down to join their lips for a brief kiss.

"I have to agree. I prefer you without any shirt at all."

"Merry Christmas, Kyla," he whispered, his throat uncomfortably tight.

"Merry Christmas, Tanner. I…uh…have a favor to ask of you." Her voice was wobbly.

He was ready to say that he had to get going, but that's not what came out.

"Anything."

"I want to go home — where I lived with my parents, I mean — just to see the place, just for a few minutes," she said, choking on the last part of her sentence.

"I think that's a great idea," he told her, though he really didn't understand why she'd want to do something like that.

"I know we don't know each other that well, but I don't

want to go there alone."

Ah, no wonder she was having a difficult time asking him. Did he really want to go along with this? It seemed too intimate, too personal — more so even than making love. He was walking away from this woman today. He started to tell her no, but once again, the wrong words came out of his mouth.

"Of course I'll go with you." What was with his brain these days?

But her sweet smile made it all worth it.

"I'm going to get changed; would it be OK if we went in half an hour?"

When he nodded, she ran back to his room, gathered her clothes, and then opened his front door, peeking out into the hall before crossing over while still wearing only his shirt. He wouldn't mind if that was all she wore the entire day.

Shaking his head, he went and grabbed a change of clothes, then jumped into the shower. She would return within minutes and he was glad, because if he had too much time to think about this, he would find a way not to go with her, and though their time together was over, he needed to grant her this one final request.

Tanner didn't know why it mattered, but he wanted her last memory of him to bring a smile to her face. If she were to hate him, he didn't think he could bear it. He was going to leave her, though, so why should her feelings matter at all?

By the time he climbed from the shower, he still didn't have any answers.

CHAPTER TWENTY-FIVE

KYLA TREMBLED AS they stood on the front porch of her family's home. The dried out and browned Christmas wreath still hung in the center of the door, testifying that this home had been a tomb for the past two years. She was so afraid to walk inside — terrified of what would be on the other side of the heavy wooden door.

"Take all the time you need."

Kyla jumped at the sound of Tanner's quiet voice. They hadn't said much at all since she'd returned to his apartment to find him ready to go. And now she'd been so lost in her thoughts that she'd forgotten his very existence.

Was this a mistake, she wondered, coming here on Christmas morning? If so, when would be the right time? If she was going to do this, now was as good a time as any.

Because her fingers were shaking too badly to insert the

house key in the lock, Tanner gently took it from her hand, set it in the keyhole, and turned. The sound of the long-unused lock clicking open seemed louder to Kyla than a rifle shot. He didn't touch the knob, just waited to see what she would do next.

With a deep, fortifying breath, Kyla opened the door. The entryway was dusty and decorated with cobwebs, the pictures on the walls barely visible under a film of grime, the floor dull with all the dust. No one had set foot in the house since a few days after the three tragic deaths, when her parents' attorney had arranged to have the food removed from the house.

He'd told her it was to keep the smell away and the rodents out. She hadn't cared about anything at that time and told him to do what he wanted. But when he'd said he would remove the Christmas decorations, too, she'd freaked out, screaming at him to leave them alone.

Later she'd apologized, but he was a kind man and had never tried to make her feel guilty about her behavior. He had offered to have a cleaning service take care of the house, but she hadn't wanted anyone inside, feeling that it would be an invasion, an insult to her mother. So the attorney had the lawn taken care of, the outside of the home looked after, but no one came inside.

Kyla's and Tanner's shoes left marks in the dust covering the floor as they walked inside, and dust motes danced around them in the thick, stale air. She found herself drawn to the family room, where a brown tree stood tall with some decorations still clinging to its brittle limbs, and some broken on the floor, the weight of the ornaments just too much over so much time. Finally, sitting beneath the once lit tree, were many wrapped gifts, all of them covered in dust.

"I'm so sorry, Kyla," Tanner whispered as he stood behind her, lifting his hand to place on her shoulder.

"This is how I feel inside — dead and broken," she said as tears welled up in her eyes.

Those gifts had been picked out with love, some of them for Kyla, some for her brother, and some for her parents.

With a few steps, she stood in front of the tree and sank down to the dirty floor, her hand reaching out as she touched one of the once brightly wrapped gifts. Picking it up, she ran her hand over the top of the package, wiping away the filth that covered its beauty.

"This one is for my brother. I got it for him. It's a football jersey for the Washington Huskies. He would have opened it and laughed, telling me there was no way he'd wear a jersey from a rival school, but he would have worn it when he got homesick. We were close, closer than most siblings. Yes, we had our fights, but we loved each other immensely. We could kick each other's asses, but if anyone else messed with either of us, we'd jump in and defend the other. I miss him so much," she said, now not making the least attempt to hide the tears.

"I don't know what to say, Kyla." Tanner just sat next to her and wrapped an arm around her.

"There's nothing to be said. It's been two years, and yet

it feels like yesterday. Why was I the one who got to live? It's not fair."

This was something she'd never said to anyone, not the therapist she'd seen for a year, not the police, not the hospital staff — not a single person. Why was she saying it now — to a stranger? Maybe because it was easier to speak with him, someone she knew she wouldn't see again when this thing between them was over.

It wasn't a matter of *if*, but of *when* it would end.

"It's Christmas. Why don't you open this?" he asked as he grabbed a small package and wiped away the dust covering the tag, showing her name clearly written in her mother's beautiful calligraphy.

"I can't," she said, though she took the package from his fingers.

"She would want you to have it."

"How do you know that? What if she just wants to be home, wants to celebrate the next fifty Christmases with her family, like she's supposed to?"

"I know she would want you to have it, because if I had a child and I died, I would watch over that kid from above, smile when they triumphed and cry when they fell. I would want my child to go on, no matter what happened. That's all any decent parent wants for their kids."

"Do you have kids?" Kyla asked, turning to look at Tanner, *really* look at him.

He paused. "No, I don't." He decided not to add that he probably never would, either.

Kyla looked down at the package, and she suddenly felt herself undoing the paper. Inside, shining up at her from a bed of velvet, was a gold heart-shaped locket with a smaller heart carved into its front.

Her fingers shaking, she opened the locket and found, staring back at her, a tiny picture of her family, one of the photos they'd had taken a month before the accident. On the opposite side was an engraved message: *We love you forever and always, Love Mom and Dad.*

Kyla smiled and sobbed and laughed at the same time as she closed the locket and struggled to open the clasp on its chain. Tanner gently eased it from her fingers and placed it around her neck.

"How can I go on?" she asked, her mouth trembling as her fingers clutched the golden heart, which rested near her own.

"You have to for your parents' and your brother's sake. They wouldn't want you to mourn them so deeply for this long. They would want you to cry, to say goodbye and then to remember them always. They would want you to live life to the fullest so the beautiful daughter and sister they loved can do all the things they wanted you to do. Weren't they happy when you succeeded?"

"Yes, my mother was my biggest cheerleader. I would call her almost every day once I moved into the dorms — after a date, after a hard test, after every little milestone. I also came home every chance I got, and she came to visit often. She was my mom and my best friend."

"Then don't you think it would tear her apart to know how much you've given up?"

Kyla thought about his words. Yes. It would rip her mother apart. She would understand that Kyla needed to mourn her family's death, but she wouldn't understand Kyla giving up living altogether. Kyla knew she had been mourning too long now.

"Thank you, Tanner. Thank you so much but I need to be here alone. I know I asked you to come, but I want to be home for a while, to feel close to my family. You can go back to the apartment now. I appreciate that you came, but I need to do this.

"Are you sure, Kyla? I don't know if I should leave you here feeling like this."

"I'm fine, Tanner. I need to say goodbye." For the first time in two years she believed that she would be okay.

"Then I'll respect that. But…"

"What, Tanner?"

"I know this isn't the time…"

Kyla looked at him levelly. "Just tell me please."

"I've had a wonderful time with you during the last three weeks; more than you could possibly imagine, and that's saying a lot for me. I don't normally spend so much time with one person – one woman, more specifically. And I need you to know that your memory will always be special to me. But you're right that I don't belong in that apartment building. And I really don't belong to anyone."

"And?"

"I don't believe I ever will. If I keep seeing you, I'd just lead you on."

"I understand, Tanner. And don't worry about it. If I can say goodbye to my parents and my brother, I can surely say goodbye to you at the same time."

Tanner stood up and helped her to her feet as he wrapped his arms around her. "Goodbye, Kyla," he said before leaning down and kissing her.

She tried to say it back, but the word wouldn't come out through her tight throat. It didn't matter. From the first moment she'd felt the connection with Tanner, she'd also known he would never be hers to hold.

Would she ever see him again, even once? When he let go, something inside of her knew this was the last time, that when she returned to the apartment building, he'd be long gone. His eyes looked regretful, but they also looked determined. She could change her mind, plead for him not to leave, but she'd known exactly how this affair would end. She'd known all along that he wasn't a person who fit into her world.

He said nothing else as he turned and left her alone in the family room. The sound of the front door opening and closing had such finality. Kyla sat back down in front of her dead Christmas tree and she wept for the last time, saying her final goodbye to her family and also to the stranger who'd come into her life to help her heal and who had left just as quietly and just as quickly as he'd shown up. Maybe he hadn't even been real at all.

CHAPTER TWENTY-SIX

THIS IS THE *life,* Tanner thought as he kicked back with a sixty-year-old scotch and looked at the snow falling outside the huge picture windows of his penthouse living room.

Home. There was no better place to be. At least there were no rodents scurrying across his floors. There were no drunks yelling outside his door, no broken water pipes or faulty heaters, and he didn't have to worry that some scumbag was going to come rushing through his door and demand money or drugs.

So why was he tense? Why was the ludicrously expensive liquor practically choking him? Why couldn't he get one woman's face from his mind? Because that place had made him temporarily insane.

Tanner stood up. He set his empty glass on the end table and paced his pristine floors, replaying the last few weeks over and over again. He'd hated being Santa, yet he couldn't erase the image of Billy asking for his parents back, saying what a good boy he would be.

Why in the hell had Judge Kragle given him such a ridiculous punishment? He would have rather spent those twenty-four days in a small jail cell. At least then he'd just be pissed off, and he wouldn't have these ridiculous what-if thoughts running through his mind.

Midnight struck and Tanner stared blankly at the antique timepiece. "Christmas is over," he said aloud, trying to get his brain to function properly. "It's over, so let's get back to the way things were."

As he climbed into bed that night, he tossed and turned, sleeping little. He should have been in ecstasy in his luxuriously oversized bed. But no, he was restless and out of sorts, feeling alone there for the first time ever.

By the time he got up the next morning, Tanner was even moodier than he'd been the night before. He'd wanted nothing more than to get back to this place for almost a whole month, but he had to get away right now. He was suffocating inside these depressingly immaculate walls. After shutting the door behind him as the sun rose in the sky, he drove to his father's office building.

At one point his dad had hoped his sons would take over the family business, and then, when none of them had stepped up to the plate, he'd sold that business and moved here, giving them each this test to turn a failing company around.

Crew had succeeded. He was doing great.

The rest of them were still struggling, fighting their father, not wanting to let the old man control them. Tanner had his own money, of course, and didn't even need to go all the way with this challenge, but he also knew that once he began something, he couldn't quit halfway through. He had to get through this task if it took everything in him. But he didn't exactly know how he'd manage that, or what the end of this game would look like, and who would be the ultimate winner.

Tanner parked in front of his father's building, then stepped inside and nodded at the guard on duty — the only other person there — before going to the elevator and riding it to the top floor. He then went into the office his father had set up temporarily for him, and he walked around. His father had given each of his kids an office in the building, hoping they'd see the light. He wanted his children to feel passion, to outgrow the selfishness they'd all embraced for a time.

Tanner felt only hollowness, as if all he had within him was a stuffing of straw. But he'd handle this. He sat down at his desk, bound and determined that this would be just a phase, a phase that would soon pass. And it would. He had a strong will, and he wouldn't be held down for long.

He thrived on work, thrived on being feared and respected for all he'd amassed. He loved glamour and power. It was all a part of who he was, and he in no way wanted to change. Three or four weeks taken from his life wouldn't make him change who he was forever. If he felt a little lonely, he could go and get a stupid cat. They weren't nearly as needy as dogs or humans.

But he wasn't an utter misanthrope. And he wasn't without some sense of family values, dammit. He would play his father's games because he did care about his family, but he certainly wasn't playing the games of some dimwitted judge. Opening his laptop, he dove into work, ignoring the fact that the rest of the building was empty, the employees spending time with their families. Holidays were no excuse for laziness. Hadn't that always been his motto?

He didn't even know anymore what he felt or what he wanted. But he would erase that thought, and he would return to normal. It might take a few more days of adjusting, but that was all. Assured he would be fine, he pushed all thoughts other than work from his mind and soon he even managed to convince himself he was perfectly okay.

He'd always been successful. Lying to himself the way he just had was proof of that.

CHAPTER TWENTY-SEVEN

W HAT DO *YOU* want, Dad?"

"Now, Tanner…"

"I'm busy now, Father. Why'd you call?"

"It's the week after Christmas," Richard told him. "And the whole family missed you at the family dinner your uncle Joseph was kind enough to include all of us in."

Tanner thought over the Christmas Eve dinner that he *had* enjoyed — immensely — and his eyes grew soft for the briefest of moments until he snapped himself out of it. That time was over, as well as it should be.

"I'd just been freed from my sentence, Dad. Did you really think I'd be in the mood to leap into the holiday spirit, to drink wassail and sing carols over a blazing fire with family love in my tender heart? That just proves how little you know about me. Anyway, I got enough Christmas spirit to choke a horse during my miserably long stint as a mall Santa."

"You didn't enjoy meeting those cute little ones?"

Tanner snorted, and then he absolutely growled. "Don't get me freaking started..." *Children!* If he never saw another one of those ankle biters again, it would be too bloody soon. Throwing up. Snot. Greed...pain... No! That last thing didn't matter. A stranger's child had no business sitting on his lap and burdening him with so much sadness. He wanted to be angry with Billy, with the world. Anger was better than vulnerability.

"Would a grown woman sound better?"

"Oh, no, Dad. Surely you're not trying to set me up with someone. The last time you got me to go out on a blind date — the only time — was the mother of all disasters."

"I'm a little more realistic now," Richard told his son. "Back then, I thought you'd want a 'nice' girl, that Melba would show you the value of...yes...personality. Don't snort at me, and don't forget that I'm still your father and always want what's best for you. Plus, I now know rather more about what men your age want and even need."

Had his dad gone round the bend? The guy hadn't even dated for years and years after Tanner's mom had departed from all their lives faster than a tired-out tornado. And now the old man was actually attempting to get a hot date for his son? Interesting. Might be worth playing along — at least for a few minutes, or until he grew bored.

"What's her name?"

"Merinda Raffel. She's the daughter of a big real estate investor in town — a friend of mine — and she needs a date tonight to take her mind off a recent disappointment. You've met her before, if I recall."

Wow. Merinda Raffel. Yes, Tanner had met her before. It was only about a month ago, at a party, and she had been endowed in all the right places. She was a true beauty. Smart, too — not just some little bimbo who would coo at him and have him ready to head for the hills before the sheets got cold. She'd been all over him, but he couldn't close on the deal because he had to get up early for his worthless trial. One of his attorneys had been at that party and had run interference, damn his hide, saying it wouldn't look good for the defendant to stand in front of Judge Kragle and look like he'd just had the debauched time of his life.

But now! Yes, now, Tanner was going to get a belated Christmas present.

"Okay, Dad, I suppose I could help you out. Not for more than this mercy operation, you know. I don't do long term. But if you want me to take her out once or twice to cheer her up, I'm sure I can take everything into hand."

"Great, son. She wants to go to a new place. It's called L'Appétit Avide."

"Of course she does. I wouldn't expect anything other than the highest pedigree of taste for a woman like Merinda."

"I thought you could afford it, Tanner, but I'd be happy to slip you the cash if you need a little help."

Crap. He'd completely forgotten that his father thought he was on the same tight budget as his siblings. He'd best be a little more careful in what and how he said certain things.

"C'mon, Dad. You know it's no problem." He delivered those words with just enough arrogance that his father surely had to ask himself what was going on. Was he wondering whether his son was covering up his insecurity about being trapped in this game with his dad as puppet master? Or was the guy unsure how he'd be able to afford the five-star meal?

Tanner expected to pay the highest of prices for his dates. It was well worth it when, at the end of the night, they kindly paid him back.

* * * * *

Merinda was certainly treating the place as if there were prizes to be won by finding the top-dollar dishes despite the built-in handicap of places like these, which had no prices on the women's menu. What would she do, Tanner asked himself, if he suggested going to get warm cookies for dessert? Or if he took her to a soup kitchen? Nah...

But he was having a good time, he tried to assure himself. All signs pointed to the sack. Her knee kept brushing his, and the gleam in her eyes and the flutter in her eyelashes told him a lot, too. She could talk with authority about caviar and wine, and when the subject turned off onto business and even the stock market, she easily kept pace with him there as well. Maybe he'd even consider a second date, at least if she was as good in bed as her looks and the heat coming off her promised.

Just as he was getting ready to suggest they take their meal to go, her eyes lit up and she looked him straight in the eye. And the conversation turned quickly for the worse.

"I couldn't help but hear about your recent sentence, Tanner." Merinda threw him a sly smile after saying what she must have been holding in all evening.

"Oh, that." He pursed his lips together, then decided to chill. Maybe she was going to actually commiserate with him and say properly nasty things about that senile judge. What was the worst she could do? They were having a great time. She wouldn't want to ruin it.

"I wish I could have seen you as Santa! I could have poked that cute little padded belly, and…"

Dammit. She was screwing with him. He should have guessed that even the most cultivated of women weren't above poking a guy while he was down. But he wasn't a wimp, or a little girl, as someone had recently suggested. He could handle this. Or he thought he could until Merinda continued.

"But, seriously, Tanner, how did you manage to live and work among the great unwashed? All those middle-class people brushing up against you in a tacky Seattle mall! And those old apartments! Have those people no shame? How can anyone live that way?"

Great unwashed? He had rubbed up against the truly unwashed on Christmas Eve. And at first he was horrified. But he'd come to know a few of them, if only a little, and to understand where they were coming from. And this woman was treating even people with homes and jobs as beneath her contempt.

"…And those awful kids, of course. Sitting on your lap! They probably drooled as they begged dear old Santa for lots and lots of the most ridiculous gifts."

No, not all of the kids were awful. Tanner could think of one in particular that he wouldn't mind seeing again. But Merinda was at last saying something sensible. He knew where this was going — she would soon launch into a denunciation of the commercialization of Christmas and the greed choking our great nation. Of course. He'd thought a bit about that over the past few weeks.

"And those kids were doubtlessly disappointed. Hell, even I was disappointed this year. Daddy is still struggling a little from the real estate bust a few years ago. And I was really eager for a decent car. My Mercedes is just so embarrassing. It's such a conservative car, really, even in price, and the darn thing is a year old now. My friends all pity me. And my wardrobe. And…"

Tanner had a lot of practice tuning this sort of thing out, and tune it out he did. What was shocking him was the fact that he was no longer so eager to take her back to his place and get her in his bed. What in the hell was wrong with him?

Who gave a crap if she was shallow? What did it matter if she was beginning to bore him? Her body was still out-of-this-world erotic, and she had lips that would fit just right around certain body parts. Strange. Why did that thought now disgust him instead of excite him?

Dinner finished a couple of long-suffering hours later,

and Tanner decided that as soon as he got the woman out of the restaurant, he'd rush her to his car, dump her at her place without so much as a goodnight kiss, and, pleading a headache, speed away.

"Tanner, you wouldn't mind making one quick stop for me, would you?" she asked, her fingernails sliding up and down his forearm, her eyes fluttering once again. He'd been interested a few hours ago, but that look was now making him physically ill.

"Of course," he said automatically, though he would rather chew on nails than spend any extra time in her presence. How had she been so interesting a month ago, and even at the beginning of their evening tonight, and then turn on him so quickly?

She named an address and Tanner's eyebrows shot together, but he pulled out into traffic and headed in that direction. When he pulled up in front of an exclusive jewelry store that was normally closed at this time of night, his pulse picked up speed.

"Oh, thanks, darling. My daddy needs me to pick up his cuff links," she said with a giggle. And she didn't move from the passenger seat.

In any other circumstance, he would have gotten out of his car and gone to open the door for her. But this time he sat there, frozen. The last thing he wanted to do was to go with her into that jewelry store.

"Tanner?" she asked.

Dammit! Caving in, he apologized for the delay before

stepping from his car and moving over to open her door.

"It's okay. I enjoy sitting in your car, too. The seats are just so comfortable, much more comfy than what I have in my outdated Mercedes."

If she made one more comment about her car, which cost more than most people made in two years, he might "accidentally" push her off the curb into oncoming traffic.

"Welcome back, Ms. Raffel. Are you here to see that necklace?"

Tanner was somehow able to wipe all expression from his face, but his body was tense as he escorted Merinda to the counter. The salesman was practically salivating. Of course he was. He worked on commission.

"No, Clinton, I'm picking up my father's cuff links," she said with a pout. But a brilliant smile turned up her lips. "But since I'm here, can I see my necklace again."

"Of course." The man went into the back and returned with a velvet case, which he set on the pristine glass counter. When he flipped open the lid, Merinda gave a happy little gasp. Then she looked up and she met Tanner's eyes with a calculating look.

He'd had enough.

Tanner had bought a lot of jewelry, and he knew it well. The necklace Merinda was so desperately trying to get him to buy her came to at least a hundred thousand dollars. That was a low-end bid. And a month ago, he'd have had no problem buying something like that if a woman was good enough in bed to be worth the high price tag.

He'd thought her beautiful. Sheesh. Now, all he could see was ugliness. How could anyone justify wearing something so extravagant for a single night when the streets were filled with people who would be grateful for a single piece of toast?

"Do you have the cuff links?" The cold authority in Tanner's voice instantly stopped the conversation that Merinda was holding with the salesman.

Her lips turned down into a pout as poor Clinton put the necklace away. And then she and Tanner exchanged not another word as he escorted her back to his car and drove her directly home. He didn't even need to plead a headache to get out of bedding this sad excuse for a woman. Her libido had frozen up when he didn't buy her that flawless diamond necklace.

By the time he got back home that night and sat down looking down upon the city, Tanner knew he was in trouble. His world was shifting, and it wasn't in a way he wanted it to shift. He only hoped it was only a temporary thing.

CHAPTER TWENTY-EIGHT

TANNER HAD NO idea why he was standing in front of this stranger's house with an armful of gifts, but standing there he was. He paced nervously as he looked at the front door and the merry wreath still hanging on it, though the holiday was now over. Finally, unable to tolerate his indecisiveness, he moved up and rang the doorbell. He heard the shuffling of feet on the other side, and he waited for the door to open.

"Can I help you?" a woman asked, looking at Tanner with suspicion.

"Is Billy home?"

"Who are you?" The woman didn't open the door any farther.

"I know him and his grandmother. They live in my building," Tanner answered. So "live" was the wrong verb tense. Close enough.

"Billy has been having a difficult time — his Christmas was so rough. I don't know if it would be a wise idea for him to see anyone right now," the woman told him.

"I can understand that, but I brought him some gifts," Tanner said. "They might help make things better."

The woman looked at him skeptically. "I can make sure he gets them," she said coolly, but she didn't back down and let Tanner in.

Tanner wanted to push past her, wanted to find Billy and tell him everything would be okay. But wouldn't he be lying? He didn't know if it would all be okay or not. He didn't seem to know anything right now other than he was a selfish bastard who'd walked away from a woman who was in deep pain and he hadn't once checked on the child the two of them had found in a basement crying and afraid. Tanner couldn't even think about seeing *Kyla,* though; he'd burned those bridges completely, all-fired jerk that he was. And so he found himself instead on Billy's doorstep, because, well, because…he didn't know the why of it.

Maybe he'd gotten the gifts for Billy to try to ease his conscience. He didn't seem to know anything anymore. One thing that he did know for sure was that this holiday season was certainly becoming his loneliest one ever.

He could have spent Christmas with his family, or at least the family that was in town, but he was too caught up in himself, in his feelings of freedom. Everyone he knew and loved was just beginning to really heal for the first time, and he hadn't had the decency to join in, to remember what

Christmas was all about.

"Thank you," he told the woman when he realized he'd been standing there too long without speaking. He handed her the gifts and turned to leave.

"I'm sure this will mean a lot to Billy."

Tanner didn't turn around and acknowledge the woman. He wasn't even sure why he'd shown up. He should have just left well enough alone and walked away from this life he'd been forced into for the past few weeks.

That's exactly what he would do. Time healed all wounds, or some crap like that. He'd heard people say it a thousand times, so didn't that mean that it had to be true? He was just going to assume it was. Feeling better already, Tanner revved up the motor on his car and decided to take a long drive. There was nothing like going over a hundred miles an hour to get your blood flowing.

He knew he was in even deeper trouble when the usual thrill he felt driving way too fast didn't happen. But he could do this. He was determined to erase the past month from his mind, and he headed toward home. He would forget Kyla and Billy too!

* * * * *

New Year's Eve.

As always, the office building had been dead, and Tanner himself felt like the walking dead — no, the sitting dead — as he stared out the window and pretended to work. Finally giving up and stepping into his sleek sports car, he started the engine. But he didn't move, and the car didn't either. He was just sitting there. He didn't want to go home to his cold condo, didn't want to be alone on yet another big holiday.

When he finally pulled out into traffic, he found himself moving in the opposite direction. Tanner crossed the long bridge onto the island one of his uncles lived on, and he soon pulled up to Joseph Anderson's colossal home.

On Christmas last year, the castle had been lit up with colored lights and it sported a giant wreath on the massive front door. And when Tanner had gone inside, he'd followed the sound of laughter coming from what he'd later learned was Joseph's favorite sitting room. Tanner had stood in the doorway and watched the activity unfolding before him.

Joseph was sitting on his huge chair, a couple of children on his lap at all times, and several more perched at his feet while he read a Christmas story. Tanner's cousins were mingling happily with his siblings, and his father could be found laughing at something his brother George said more often than not. That was last year.

Tanner had missed all of that this year. The decorations he saw outside the mansion now weren't about joy to the world. They were about endings and beginnings. The excitement was of a different sort. Did he really want to face this? He thought seriously of turning around and leaving, but that didn't happen. He walked from his car and moved up to the front steps.

Once again he followed the sound of laughter, and this

time he was in the big ballroom, with masses of balloons overhead. Those balloons seemed oppressive enough in his dark mood, but even more upsetting was what was beneath them.

Seeing the couples locked in each other's arms was too much for Tanner, who suddenly felt more alone than he could ever remember feeling. And that made no sense. He didn't need another person in his life to make him happy — he hadn't felt that way for years, not since his childhood — so he didn't understand this absurd sense of sadness that seemed to be washing through him.

He'd made a mistake in coming to this place. He turned around, planning to sneak back out before anyone spotted him. But he was too late.

"Tanner! I can't believe you actually made it!" Crew was quickly approaching, his beautiful wife, Haley, sweetly glued to his side.

"I'm so glad you did," Haley said. "We really missed you at Christmas, but I figured the ladies' man would be too busy with his lady friends." She detached herself from her husband, threw her arms around Tanner, and gave him a big hug.

"Tanner doesn't go for *ladies*, exactly," Crew said. "He likes his women a little more down and dirty."

"Shut up, Crew. It's good to see you again, Haley." He turned to his brother when she released him. "I'm not staying long. I just thought I would stop by, bro."

"Oh, nonsense," Crew said. "What in the world is

more important during the *whole* Christmas season than family? Better late than never. Anyway, we're just about to have dinner. And there are a few single ladies nearby who wouldn't mind giving you a kiss at midnight to ring in the New Year." After nudging Tanner in the back, Crew led him to the bar and had a drink poured for him.

For the first time in what felt like at least a week, Tanner's lips twitched. He knew without a doubt that there was one single lady who wouldn't let him get his lips anywhere near hers, no matter what time of the year it was, and no matter how many other couples were kissing all around them.

Tanner had gone back to the jeweler and purchased the box Merinda's necklace was in. And then he'd written her a note — a clever note, if he did say so himself. He could almost — almost, but not quite — picture the rage flaring up in her eyes when that lid came open and she read his words. He'd simply placed an identical plastic necklace in the box, one designed for a child, and thanked her for reminding him about the true meaning of Christmas. A donation in the amount of one hundred fourteen thousand dollars was being donated to the Seattle Mission, the exact cost of the necklace she'd more than hinted that she wanted.

His only regret was that he wouldn't be there to see her face. His mood did instantly improve, though, just thinking about it. Enough that he accepted the glass his brother had brought him and he downed it, delighting in the slow burn of fine scotch as it traveled down his throat. He got another one and sipped away contentedly as more family members found him.

"How was your stay at that old apartment building?" his cousin Mark asked.

"It was awful," Tanner replied. "I've never been so happy to leave a place. That judge was seriously out of his mind."

"It couldn't have been too awful, not with such a hot neighbor," Lucas said with a wink.

"A hot neighbor? Something you want to tell me about?" Lucas's wife, Amy, added a teasing smile to her question.

"Well, of course she didn't even come close to comparing to you," Lucas said before grabbing Amy and kissing her, making her giggle.

"Hey, kids. Save it for midnight," Tanner grumbled.

"Oh, you're just jealous," Crew retorted as he planted a kiss on his own better half.

"Ha! I don't want the marriage-and-kids thing. I like my freedom way too much," Tanner said. He finished his second glass of scotch and went back for more.

"Yeah, that's what we all said," Lucas told his cousin. "I've certainly changed my mind about that."

"It seems all the good women have been snatched up already, so I'll just have to deal with my sad bachelorhood status," Tanner said, breaking out an arrogant smile, and hoping it came through just fine. "Or did I mean revel in it?"

"The harder they fight, the more it hurts when they fall," Joseph said in his booming voice as he joined them.

"Happy New Year, Uncle Joseph," Tanner said. He'd only known this man for about a year, but the guy was larger than life and Tanner couldn't imagine anyone on the whole planet who didn't instantly love him.

"Happy New Year to you, too, Tanner. I'm sure glad you decided to show your face. I was a little offended you weren't here last week," Joseph said in his gruff manner, making Tanner feel instantly like a child who was being scolded. "But you must be so glad to see the last of that apartment and those kids in the mall. At least that's what your father said would happen."

"It wasn't all bad."

"No?"

"There was someone I met who was really nice. Maybe two people. And I worry about them. But there's nothing I can do to help either of them. Not now."

Tanner didn't even realize he was going to say any of that until it popped from his mouth. Who in the hell was he? When he finished speaking, though, he was surprised to see a gleam in his father's eyes. Those couldn't possibly be tears.

"You have grown a lot this past year, son. I'm proud of you," Richard said.

"You might feel that there's nothing you can do, Tanner, but you'd be surprised by what can happen when you put your mind to it," Joseph added.

Tanner shifted uncomfortably on his feet and was relieved when the topic changed. Still, he couldn't get Kyla from his mind, or Billy, for that matter. Amid all the laughter, he felt even more alone than ever before.

Nonsense!

Pulling himself together, he managed to hold on until the countdown began for the new year. But as he looked out at his relatives, all of them with someone, all happy and in love — or at least that's the way it appeared to him — he decided he'd had enough. He wasn't going to watch others lips lock together, not when there was only one woman he wanted to kiss this New Year's Eve. And it wasn't going to happen.

It didn't matter, though, because he was happy with his life, he told himself, refusing to cave in to the depression hanging threateningly overhead.

Kyla was from his past and there was no use in turning back.

CHAPTER TWENTY-NINE

TANNER KNEW HE'D lost his mind when he found himself parked in front of the old apartment building a week into the new year. This was the place where he'd been condemned to live for more than three weeks while donning a Santa suit and dealing with a bunch of whiny kids. Why in the world was he subjecting himself to coming back here?

Because this is where Kyla lived, and he couldn't stop thinking about her.

Two full weeks had passed since he'd left her there alone in her parents' home, and she'd looked so lost and broken. Should he have stayed? Yes, he felt like a heel for not waiting for her on the front steps. And like a worse heel for actually breaking up with her on the spot. He'd been trying to be kind, but... He snorted. Kind? *Scared* was more like it.

What if she'd needed him once she'd stepped outside that

mausoleum of a home?

He'd just taken her at her word and left. Called a cab and rushed back to his old life. He hadn't even bothered going back to the apartment building. There was nothing there he'd needed or wanted.

Nothing but Kyla.

He was just going to check on her now. Nothing more. He'd slept with her, after all; it was the responsible thing to do to make sure she was doing well. Just because he wanted to check on her didn't mean he cared, or that he wanted to have an actual relationship.

He didn't do relationships. For the past several years, he'd found women who were interested in mutually beneficial sex. That was great — no one got feelings hurt when it was over, usually after one night in bed, maybe two.

Still, he found himself striding down the hallway of the building. As he moved toward Kyla's door, he was beginning to see the place differently. Maybe there really were some possibilities here. As much as he didn't want to think it, there was beauty in the moldings and now that the heating was working properly and the place was getting much-needed repairs, he could see some potential. He'd have to meet with his architect.

Tanner found himself in front of Kyla's door, and his hand went on autopilot. Hell, it wasn't the first time that had happened. Footsteps on the other side told him she was home.

With the chain in place, she cracked the door open.

He would have to tell her that wasn't a surefire method of keeping people out. Once they had an opening, no matter how small, they could easily force their way in.

"Hello, Kyla." Hell. Was he an expert on doing lame?

She must have thought so, because she left the door chained. "What are you doing here, Tanner?"

"I missed you." Tanner didn't know which of them was more surprised by his words.

"You disappeared," she said. Her look was clear: *Don't think you have a chance at a repeat of our night together, Tanner. You had your chance, and you lost it.*

"I was only ever going to be living here for three or four weeks. But it was an…experience," he said, pasting on his most charming smile. "Why don't you invite me in?"

"I don't understand. Who moves into a place for only that little stretch of time?" The door shut as she unlatched the chain. She opened her door wider, but she blocked the opening, letting him know that he definitely wasn't being invited inside.

"It's a long story and I don't want to get into it," he told her.

"Everything seems to be a long story to you. You seem to love keeping your secrets. That's fine with me, Tanner, because I don't see that we really have anything to talk about. You moved in, we had sex, you moved on. It's pretty much the end of our story."

Though she was trying to be flippant, he could see the hurt behind her eyes and in her voice. Kyla wasn't the type of woman a man slept with and then left with only a few words and no explanations. He'd known that all along, and yet he'd still done it. He was the type of man mothers warned their daughters about.

The thought didn't sit well with him.

"I would like to take you out on a real date, Kyla. If you come with me, I'll tell you more of my story."

"I don't think so, Tanner. I just…I don't think we have anything in common."

"We sure had a lot in common on Christmas Eve," he said, leaning toward her, taking in her sweet scent and instantly flooded with desire for her. Even without makeup and wearing sweats, she turned him on far more than his last supermodel had during their one-night stand.

"That's sex, Tanner. There's a difference between having good sex and having a relationship. Does that come as a surprise to you? No, I didn't think so. We both knew when we slept together that it wasn't going to lead into anything more. So I expected not to sleep with you again. But I didn't expect you to completely disappear."

"You said you wanted to be alone," he said in a helpless effort at self-defense.

"I did. Thank you for respecting that."

"Have you made any decisions?"

"Not yet. I spoke to my parents' attorney. I think I'm going to sell the house. I just can't stay there. It would hurt too badly, and the place I loved needs to have people in it who will create their own happy memories. I want to wait until

I'm sure, however; I don't want to do anything rash."

"I think that's wise. But it's time for you to start living again."

"Yes, I agree, which is why I spoke to the admissions office at my old college this week. I'm hoping to get back to school for spring term, though I'm cutting it close. I'll have to see if it works out."

"That's wonderful, Kyla." Shockingly, he actually meant it.

"I think you should go now, Tanner. It's been nice seeing you, though." She tried to shut the door, but he blocked it with his hand.

"Please. I just want to talk, Kyla." What the hell? He wasn't the kind of guy to beg a woman for attention.

Before she could respond, there were footsteps in the hallway, and as Tanner moved around to see who was coming, he heard his name being called.

"Mr. Storm, I'm so glad to find you here. The demolition crew is going back through the building for a new plan to turn into the city, and they need your signature on some papers."

Tanner turned back just in time to watch Kyla's eyes widen when reality hit. He knew his chances of getting her to speak to him had just flown completely out the window. His team had told him that they were getting new bids on various costs for what to do with the building, but he hadn't realized they'd be working as soon as today. For a man whose luck was nearly perfect — could that be only in finance? — today was turning out not to be his day.

"You own this building?" she gasped.

Unless he was prepared to make up a story and lie outright, Tanner was caught. "My father handed it over to me six months ago."

Her eyes narrowed dangerously. "So you're the worthless bastard who's been trying to evict us since you got your greedy hands on the place. What were you doing here, Tanner — or should I say *Mr. Storm*? Were you scoping out the place, hoping to find proof that it needed to be condemned so you could rip it all down and then come in and build some fancy high-rise?"

At his guilty look, her eyes narrowed even more, if that were possible.

"That's what I thought. I am *such* a fool. I knew you were out of my league. I could practically smell it on you, but I had no idea how far out you really were. Did you have fun slumming it with a poor girl down on her luck? You must have really wanted to close the deal — after all, you subjected yourself and your manicured hands to serving food at a homeless shelter."

"It wasn't like that," he said, running his fingers through his hair in frustration.

"I know exactly how it was, Tanner. You were stuck here doing your underhanded snooping, and I just happened to be in front of you. With nothing better on the horizon, you decided to get an easy lay. I'm sorry it took so long. Hell, if I had turned over sooner and hadn't had that attack of shame, you could have gotten more than just a *couple* of nights of cheap sex." Tears filled her eyes, but she refused to let them fall.

"I was forced to be here by a judge! I wasn't spying," he snapped as he paced in front of her.

Residents who'd been approaching heard danger and wisely backed away, though not so far that they couldn't overhear all of this juicy information.

"Oh, I see. That makes it so much better. You're some rich guy who committed a crime and got community service instead of jail time. That's why you were Santa, isn't it?"

He nodded, though before he could try to defend himself again, she said what was clearly her final piece.

"You need to keep away from me. I don't ever want to see you again." Before he could stop her, she slammed the door shut and he was left standing there wondering what the hell had just happened.

When pounding on her door didn't get a response, he turned away. She wasn't going to speak to him again. It was no use. As he walked past a small group of men he saw standing at the end of the hall, the expression on his face dared them to say a word. Luckily for them, they kept silent.

When Tanner left the building, his car peeled out, tires squealing. He was furious with Kyla, furious with the whole situation. By the time he got home, he'd calmed down, but he couldn't help his unbelievable frustration as he walked through his rooms.

How could he make this better? What would make this ache go away? No answers there. He just laughed bitterly when he joked to himself about opening up his little black book of hot models. He knew they'd jump at the chance to satisfy him — as if any one of them could come close. He didn't have the least desire to see any one of them again, under any circumstance. So instead, he went off to bed, hoping that by the time he woke up, he'd have some idea how to make this all right.

He was Tanner Storm. He would figure this out.

CHAPTER THIRTY

T ANNER SIGNED THE last of the documents and sat back with a genuine smile. He knew he was doing the right thing, because he felt good about himself. The last time he could remember feeling like this was when…hell, he couldn't remember having this feeling before.

"Sir, it's time to head out to the news conference."

"I'll be leaving in a moment," he told his secretary. He handed her the sheaf of papers and stood up.

He whistled as he made his way to the elevators and rode downstairs. With luck, he would be seeing Kyla today. He in no way expected her to give in easily, but wasn't that part of the fun in all of this?

For the first time in his life, he was enjoying the chase, enjoying that there was a woman out there who wasn't afraid to tell him what she really thought. And he wanted to be with this woman, not just for a night of passion, or ten nights of passion for that matter, but for the kind of time that ended after forever.

He slipped into the backseat of the waiting car along with his assistant and thought of only one thing as the driver wove through the heavy Seattle traffic — seeing her again. If all went well, he'd soon have her in his arms. He couldn't expect it too quickly, of course. It certainly wouldn't happen tonight. But he'd stick with his pursuit of her for as long as it took. She was worth it.

A crowd was waiting in front of the apartment building as he emerged from the car. Reporters were asking questions; cameras flashed. He smiled, waved and continued forward, stepping up on the podium that had been set up for this event.

Tanner waited for the crowd to quiet down, and then he spoke. "When I received this building from my father, I didn't look at it — really look at it. I just saw dollar signs, with an old building standing in my way. I didn't look at the architecture, at the historic value. But a woman who lives here helped me to see it through new eyes. That is why I have decided to renovate this beautiful piece of history in a city that I've come to love. The project will take two years to complete, but when we are finished, this apartment building will stand proud, regaining all her former glory. And I'll be proud, too. The residents who live here will have a home as long as they want, and we will keep the costs down for those who move in when we're finished fixing the place up. I want to thank my father, a very wise man, for showing me that the bottom line isn't what counts above everything else, but that having justifiable pride in oneself is just as important — in fact, more important. He believed that the restoration of this building would remind me of who I am. And he was right."

"Mr. Storm! Mr. Storm!" Hands shot up as every one of the reporters tried to get his attention.

"Yes?" he said, pointing to a freckle-faced young reporter, a young Jimmy Olsen who seemed ecstatic to be the first one picked.

"Who is the woman? Could there be a romance involved?"

Tanner was quiet for a moment. He smiled and looked out into the crowd and locked eyes with Kyla. Oh yes, there was a romance, at least if he had anything to say about it.

"I sure hope so," he said, a huge grin splitting his face, and a gasp surged through the crowd. The reporters shouted out more and more questions, but Tanner tuned them all out and let Randy handle things. He only had eyes for one person right now and she was giving him an assessing look. He could see that she didn't trust him, was leery of his motives. But he'd expected that. He was here to show her that his intentions were pure.

After the reporters had what they needed, he stepped down and shook hands, searching for any sign of Kyla. She was apparently long gone, but that was all right with him. He would be here a lot over the next several months. Tanner had decided to don his construction hat and work on the building himself, along with the prestigious firm he'd hired for the project. If Crew could do this kind of thing, he most certainly could, too.

CHAPTER THIRTY-ONE

TWO WEEKS DRAGGED by, and though Tanner spotted Kyla often, she always walked past him without a word. A few times, he'd seen the way some of the crew checked her out; after a stern look from him, they'd soon backed off. He had no trouble at all with letting them know she was off limits. Even if she didn't know it yet, she was his and he wasn't letting her go.

It hit him like a flash flood one afternoon when he was up on a ladder and she went by him in the hall. It was like a picture show in his mind — the two of them laughing in her kitchen, holding each other on the couch, her falling asleep in his arms… He'd tumbled headfirst into love with this woman, this beautiful, tragic, compelling woman.

Everything he was doing was because she'd changed forever the way he thought about his life. She'd changed his thinking for the better. What the…? *It's a Wonderful Life* was turning into his reality.

Now, he just had to persuade her to give him another chance, to let him love her. No, he had no idea how the hell he was going to manage to do that. But with new determination, he climbed down the ladder, set down his hammer, walked to her door, and pounded on it.

"Open up, Kyla," he yelled through her door. "I have something to say and I refuse to leave until you hear me out." He didn't even even notice that the noise in the hall had stopped as his workers unabashedly listened in as their boss prepared to play the lovesick fool.

"Go away, Tanner. We have nothing to say to each other."

"Dammit, if you don't open this door, then I'm going to shout it all out for the neighbors to hear!"

"There are children here, Mr. Storm. You watch your language."

Tanner turned to find one of the neighbors' doors open and an older woman glaring daggers at him. But he didn't care who listened in. He wasn't leaving until he got what he had to say off his chest. Hell, he wasn't leaving without carrying Kyla away in his arms.

Considering he'd lied to her and had wanted only to use her for her body, then walked away as if she meant nothing, he figured he had to perform some penance. Maybe more than a little. But whatever it took, he would do it, even if that meant groveling.

"Granted, I didn't tell you who I was. I lied by omission, Kyla, and I admit I wanted to get you into my bed more than anything else. I was selfish, shortsighted, and a complete idiot. It took spending three or four of the most meaningful weeks of my life with you to realize how foolishly I was behaving. I should have never left you on Christmas. I should have waited on your doorstep and then held you all night as you let out your grief. I'm begging you to give me another chance to do just that."

"Tanner…you have to stop this," she said, sounding choked up, sounding…hopeful?

Was he actually getting through to her?

"Please, just let me prove to you that I'm a new man. I know some men say they will change when they have zero intention of doing so, but I *have* changed. I'm a better man for knowing you, and I want to prove to you every single day how much I care — how much I love you. I do, Kyla Ridgley. I love you so much, my heart is bursting."

The onlookers gave out a muted *awww*.

But Kyla's door stayed shut, although he kept staring at it, willing it to open.

"Please, just open the door, Kyla. Look into my eyes. You'll see that I'm telling the truth!"

"You're making a fool of yourself, young man," said the woman down the hall. But the look she now gave him was far less harsh than the one she'd treated him to before. She seemed almost sympathetic to his plight.

That hurt, he had to admit. He knew things were bad when he was getting pitying looks from elderly women.

Finally, just when he thought he was going to have to

pitch a tent outside Kyla's door, he heard her undoing the locks and sliding the chain away. Then she was standing before him, looking even more beautiful than ever, with her hair in a ponytail, and wearing a tight red sweater and a pair of fitted jeans that showed off the perfect flare of her hips.

Tears were shining in her eyes as she gazed into his. He could see myriad emotions crossing her features, as if she were hoping he spoke the truth, but didn't trust herself to be a good judge of his character.

"I'm such a fool, Kyla. But I'm a man who will only make a mistake once before I've learned my lesson. I know we haven't had a lot of time together, and I know it all seems like it moved too fast, but since I've been away from you, you're all I think about. I can't concentrate on work; I can hardly sleep, or eat. I'm just surviving, not living. I need you as a part of my life — a permanent part of my life. I won't terrify you by asking you to be my wife…at least not today… but I am asking for a chance, a real chance for us to know each other. I love you, Kyla. I've never before said that to a woman."

"Oh, Tanner, I…I don't know. My first instinct is to throw my arms around you and say yes, but this is too fast. We don't know each other. We spent less than a month together and…" She dropped her voice briefly to a whisper. "We made love only twice. I want to believe this is real, but things like this don't happen to somebody like me. You're a man who has the world in the palm of his hand. I'm just a lost girl, someone who's pretty much alone in this world, and I have nothing to bring to the relationship," she said, hugging herself tightly.

"How can you say that? You are *everything*, Kyla. You're strong and beautiful, funny and caring. You have a heart of gold. Though you've been dealt some difficult cards in life, that doesn't define who you are; it only shows how much strength you actually have. I fell in love with you because of your strength and your goodness and…everything about you. Please let me prove to you how much." He reached out and gently pried her arms away from her body so he could take her hands into his.

"I…I stopped believing in love when I lost my family," she said, the pain so clear in her eyes that he felt it to his very soul.

"Then let me show you how to love again."

She allowed him to fold her into his arms, and she rested her head against his chest and sobbed. A flood of emotions she'd been holding in for so long broke free, and he was strong enough to carry her through.

"Please just let me love you, Kyla. I promise to cherish you, promise to help you carry the burden you've been carrying alone for too long."

"I love you too, Tanner. I don't know when or how, but I've missed you, missed your smile and your jokes, missed the way I felt when I was with you. The pain faded, hid away for a while when I was with you. I think I felt guilty about that, felt as if it were wrong for me to keep living my life, to be happy when the rest of my family couldn't be here to experience such wonderful emotions. I know now that's not what they would want. I know they'd want me to be happy."

"Yes, they would," he said, and leaned down and captured her lips.

As he kissed her, his heart flooding with love, he suddenly noticed the clapping. Lifting his head, he looked around and saw the hall filled with people who had just witnessed his groveling. But he didn't even care. The old Tanner would have, but he was a new man. Hadn't he said that much to the world?

"Congratulations, sonny," the nosy neighbor said, then went back into her apartment now that the show was over.

The construction workers didn't move.

"Get back to work," Tanner told them, trying to sound stern, but not able to pull it off, since he couldn't get the goofy grin from his face.

"Let's have some privacy," Kyla said, pulling away and holding out her hand for him to take.

She didn't have to tell him twice.

The two entered her apartment, and he couldn't believe how nervous he was. He couldn't mess this up now that she'd finally let him in.

"I don't want you to think this is about sex, but I want you so badly," he said, unable to quit running his hands up and down her back.

"It's definitely about sex. I want you too, Tanner," she admitted, then pressed up against him and kissed him with a hunger that could only match his.

Lifting her up into his arms, he carried her to her room

and stood her in front of her bed, slowly taking off each piece of her clothing, his fingers shaking as he bared her body to his enraptured eyes. After laying her gently on the covers, he yanked off his own clothes without taking his eyes from her.

Then he climbed up on top her, lying between the perfect heat of her thighs, and he kissed her again, enjoying the slow tangling of their tongues as they reacquainted themselves with each other.

He moved his head down her neck, sucking her skin and rejoicing in her taste. After skimming his lips across the tender mounds of her breasts, he proceeded to her stomach, enjoying the quiver in her belly while rested his chest against her core.

Lightly, he kissed her stomach while he caressed her sides and arms, her skin a perfect silk beneath his rough hands. Bringing his arms beneath her, he lifted her up and moved lower, cherishing this moment.

She pushed up against him, her body knowing exactly what it needed, and slowly, inch by mesmerizing inch, he approached her very center, letting his tongue trace the sexy bone of her hip and then going to where her heat was calling him.

The quiet moan escaping her throat floated around him and made his body throb with even greater need. He pressed his lips downward, then fluttered kisses on the soft folds of her womanhood.

Lifting one of her legs, he placed it on his shoulder, opening her fully up to him so he could gaze at her perfection before leaning down and tasting her again, exciting her, building her pleasure to nearly unbearable levels.

Unable to take it slow any longer, he kissed her heat intimately, worshipping her beautiful folds with his hot tongue and making her cry out when he sucked her swollen bud into his mouth and swiped his tongue across it.

"Tanner, please take me," she gasped out, and though he wanted to sink within her, he also wanted to keep drinking her in, feeling her, making her burn.

His arousal pulsed with incredible need, and he reached down and gripped it, trying to ease the ache. It didn't help. It had been too long since he'd been inside her, and his body remembered all too well how good she felt.

But Tanner continued to tease her, at first slowly, and then with growing speed, kissing, licking and sucking her tender flesh until he felt her tense, felt her body find the release he'd been taking his sweet time building for her.

When he slipped his finger inside her, the walls of her womanhood pulsed around him, and her wet heat showed him she wanted more, needed to have him inside of her.

When the last of her tremors died down, he let his tongue caress her core one last time, enjoying that her taste had become even more exquisite than before, and her hips pushed upward, seeking him.

"Please, Tanner," she begged.

He thought he wasn't going to deny the two of them any longer. But as he kissed his way back up her flawless body, he had to stop at her hardened peaks and suck each into his mouth while holding the other one, his fingers pinching and teasing, making her gasp and pant and moan.

Finally, their bodies were lined up, his arousal pressed against her, and he looked down into her eyes, feeling that he could get lost there forever, feeling that he was finally home.

"I love you, Kyla, love you more than I ever imagined anyone could love. I know I said I wouldn't bring up marriage, I know I said this was too soon, but when you know something is right, you just know. I want you to be my wife. I want to spend the rest of my life with you — making love, laughing, crying, learning and growing. I never want to spend another night without you. Please let me have you forever."

Kyla's eyes widened. "It's too soon," she said, though there was no conviction in her voice.

"Don't worry about what anyone else thinks. Just tell me what you want," he said, pushing forward the slightest bit, connecting their bodies together, but just barely.

"I want you," she said, her head turning as she tried to push up closer, to have more of him — all of him — inside her.

"Forever," he demanded, driving in another inch, the torture nearly undoing him.

"Forever," she conceded.

With that one word, he thrust deeply inside of her, and their cries mingled together as they became one. There was no more talking now. He lifted them both higher and higher, built their pleasure and then spilled his seed within her.

By the time their passion was spent and he was holding her in his arms, caressing her skin and thanking heaven that he'd seen the light, Tanner could barely hold his eyes open. But he did have one final thought.

If he ever ran into Judge Kragle again, he'd probably have to tell him that he was a pretty good guy. The man had altered Tanner's life for the better.

On second thought, why encourage such a meddling old guy? Tanner decided that he probably wouldn't admit a thing.

He'd just think it when he finally came up for air.

EPILOGUE

"WE JUST HAVEN'T had a miss yet, have we, brother?"

Joseph looked at his brother George with a smile. "Of course we haven't. We are Andersons after all," he said with a boisterous laugh.

"I sure missed out growing up with the two of you, but I think I'm learning quite well on my own," Richard said as he sat back with a big grin.

"Oh yes, brother. You may be named Storm, but the Anderson blood runs through your veins hot and fast," Joseph told him proudly.

"I knew the minute I met Kyla in that old building that she was perfect for one of my boys," Richard said. "To tell you the truth, I thought she'd be well suited for Lance, but she and Tanner are a perfect match."

"Yes, they are, and now that they have adopted Billy,

they've already begun their family," George said.

"I should get some credit here," Judge Kragle said with a hearty laugh of his own.

"Sentencing him to community service and to stay in his building was pure genius. You get ninety percent of the credit," Richard told him.

"And don't forget what my granddaughter did to push Tanner in the right direction," the judge added. "Merinda's acting classes really paid off. Do you think your boy will ever figure it all out?"

"Hopefully not. If he does, I think we're all in for it," George said, pretending to wipe sweat from his brow.

"I'm not too worried. Plus, Merinda said she busted up laughing when that jewelry box arrived with the plastic necklace and his note in it. She said it was the best gift she's ever received, knowing that so many more people would have warm meals because of her acting skills."

"Ah, how could he be upset even if he knew? Love blossomed for that boy, and he's happier than he's ever been," Richard told them confidently.

"That's true. Those children of ours just don't appreciate how much effort and energy we put into their happiness," Joseph groused. "We never get thank-yous or gratitude of any kind. And just look at all the beautiful children they've produced so far."

"They just think we're meddling old men," George said. "Someday, when their own children are all grown, they'll come to appreciate us more."

"I wouldn't go quite that far — these youngsters can be mighty ornery — but you don't need thanks from them," Kragle replied. "Having all of those grandchildren is thanks enough."

"I still wouldn't mind a thank-you," Joseph growled. This had been something he'd been saying for years, but though he could bark with the best of him, he wasn't the type to bite.

"So who's next?" Kragle asked, eagerly joining the three brothers in their matchmaking schemes.

"I've been seeing some big changes in Ashton of late. I think it's time to focus our attention on him now," Richard said, accepting another glass of scotch.

"Well, then, Ashton it is," George said, clinking glasses with his brother.

"And I want in," Kragle said with a chuckle.

"We won't turn you down," Joseph said.

The four men bent their heads together and the scheming continued…

**Read the beginning of the Anderson /
Storm Saga with Lucas's story, *The Billionaire
Wins the Game*, available now.
Coming Soon, the next book in
Anderson / Storm Series**

If you enjoyed Holiday Treasure, you might want to check out Melody Anne's brand new book in her *Forbidden* series:

BOUND

Read on for an excerpt, coming up next

PRELUDE

TAKE OFF YOUR clothes."

Jewell looked at Blake as if he'd lost his mind. "What?"

His eyes narrowed. "Take off your clothes. Do not make me repeat myself again." He stood back and looked at her through silver eyes that seemed to see right into her soul.

"I c…can't. We're in a parking garage," she stammered. She looked desperately around at the full lot.

Sure, this corner happened to be dark, but what if someone drove in? What if a police car cruised by again? There was no way she could do what he was ordering her to.

Blake just waited in silence, leaning against the front of his car and watching her pace nervously in front of him.

"Please?" Sheesh. She was reduced to begging now.

"I guess our agreement is finished, then." He shrugged as if he didn't care.

Was he bluffing? Could she take the chance? Her stomach knotted painfully as she weighed her options.

Wanting more than anything to walk away, she closed her eyes and saw her brother's sweet, impish face. What was she willing to do for him?

Anything.

CHAPTER ONE

I'M PLEASED WE'RE now business partners. I think this venture will be a success."

Blake Knight laughed as he shook hands with Rafe Palazzo, gratified that the man had finally come to visit from San Francisco. Though Blake had known Rafe for many years, this was the first project the two of them had paired up on. The contracts were signed, and the deal would put a few more hundreds of millions into both of their already fat wallets.

"I don't think there's a venture out there with your name on it that isn't a success, Rafe."

"Ah, my friend, the same can be said about what you and your brothers do," Rafe replied without missing a beat.

"We're just that damn good, I guess," Blake said.

Though at first glance the two of them might come off as smug and self-satisfied, and they might look at multimillion-dollar investments the same way an average person looked at depositing twenty dollars into their savings account, the men were shrewd and their self-assessments were based on solid fact, not ego. They knew how to make money, and they knew they'd always keep making more.

Only a select few ruled the world, and when Blake Knight was a young boy and his parents' lives ended right before his very eyes, he'd decided right then that he would never be vulnerable again. He would never be one of the weak, never be easy prey to a world packed with predators. No one would sneak up on him and catch him unawares.

"Let's have a drink, and you can fill me in on what you've been doing for the past year," Rafe told Blake. "Too much time has gone by since our last visit."

The two of them moved toward the conference room doors at Knight Construction.

"You're the one who sold your soul to a woman and disappeared," Blake reminded his friend.

"Don't knock it, Blake. Ari has changed my life and made me a better man."

"Oh, please, *please*, for the love of all that's holy, do not continue," Blake said, horrified to hear these words coming from a man who was once one of the most ruthless bachelors he'd ever met. "I remember the days when you thought no woman was true, no woman could ever be trusted. Marriage — your second marriage — has ruined you. There's a term for it, you know…"

"There was a time, Blake, when I would have thrown you

up against a wall for just thinking me the slightest bit weak."

"Ha! You would have tried," Blake said.

Neither of them was remotely upset by the exchange, of course. It was all friendly banter.

Rafe smiled and spoke reflectively. "I came to realize that the anger I'd held onto for too long was pointless. I also realized that having one woman to love didn't end my life or my freedom. It made everything better. Ari is full of surprises and delights that I'll never get tired of exploring. I know you'll scoff at such talk, but what she does for me is indescribable."

"Yeah, whatever, Rafe — and thanks for not describing it. I happen to be a big fan of variety. After a few weeks, anything gets old, and women are no exception. I always grow bored with them — always! Besides, though I know it's not politically correct to say this, face it: women are weak, pathetic creatures, and they always have an agenda. Once I've broken their spirit, there's no more fun to be had with the relationship."

Rafe knew the horror that Blake and his brothers had suffered together when their mother's little game hadn't ended the way she'd wanted it to end. The woman had hardened his friend's heart, and though Blake was letting his resentment toward one woman carry over to all of them, it was somewhat understandable, if not right or rational. Hell, Rafe had done the same thing after his first wife's betrayal. So he knew there was hope. Time would eventually change Blake because he was fundamentally a good man.

"Not every woman is like your mother, Blake. You'll see that someday." Before Blake could say anything, Rafe went off on a slight tangent. "Who are you seeing now?"

The two men had made it to the lobby of the building and were stepping out onto a busy Seattle sidewalk. They were heading toward a favorite bar of Blake's.

"No one at the moment. I just haven't had time — all of these deals to be closed. You know the drill. And I've had to do a lot of the work here on my own, what with my brother Byron being off in Greece for the past year, and my other brother, Tyler, gone two years. Now that they are home, I may take some vacation time."

"Now that's a joke. Men like us don't do vacations," Rafe said. "Why were both your brothers away?"

"Byron was working on his own project in Greece. He was working with me on deals for the home front," Blake replied.

"It's good to branch out on your own sometimes, Blake. I would like to hear more about this from him. I personally love spending time in Greece. A beautiful country."

"Yeah, and Tyler was just gone for two years—we don't know where. And we didn't hear from him. I was about to send out the marines, but he finally came home."

"Now that sounds like a story," Rafe said.

Before Blake was able to give Rafe any details, the two men were interrupted.

"Rafe. Blake. How are you?"

Blake turned to look at Mathew Greenfield, a man who'd

helped him through more than one bad time in his life. He was a business partner, but more than that, he'd been there when Blake had needed to choose which road he was going to take in life.

Luckily, Blake had taken a more positive path than the one he'd originally thought he would. And Mathew had given him the support and praise he needed to change his life for the better — no easy feat, under the circumstances.

Mathew also knew all of Blake's dark secrets, and he was still someone Blake could not only count on, but trust fully, too.

"It's good to see you, my friend," Blake said.

"It's been a long time," Rafe told Mathew.

"Too long," Mathew replied.

"Join us for a drink," Blake said. "We're celebrating a new business venture." He knew Rafe wouldn't mind.

Mathew threw him a smile. "I have a few minutes. Why don't you tell me about it?"

The three men walked into the bar and proceeded to the back, where Blake had a table on standby at this same time every day in case he needed to conduct business away from the offices. A waitress quietly set down menus and disappeared.

Once the topic of business was out of the way, the conversation turned back to Blake's lack of a love life. That didn't make him a happy camper, especially since the last people on earth he'd want to discuss this with were teaming up on him.

"We all need to take time to have our itches scratched," Mathew said with a knowing look. "Have you heard of Relinquish Control?"

"What in the hell is that?" Blake asked with disdain.

"It's a place where you can get your needs met — discreetly," Mathew replied.

Rafe looked skeptical. "I haven't heard of it, and I'm not sure I want to."

"That's because you're a very happily married man who doesn't need a specialty escort service. It's only a couple of years old now, but there hasn't been a single complaint from any of the clients."

"I've never had trouble getting my needs met, and anyway...," Blake said just before the waitress dropped off their appetizers and new drinks.

"Yeah, but sometimes a man is just too damn busy. Relinquish might still be fairly new, but it's run by a very good friend of mine, and I promise you, you won't regret checking it out."

"Sorry, but there's no way in hell I'm going to a place like that."

"Well, here's their card in case you change your mind."

Mathew held out a nondescript white business card, and for some odd reason, Blake not only accepted it, but also found himself slipping it into his pocket. He told himself it was so he wouldn't offend a good friend and colleague. But as soon as he got home, he'd chuck the card into the trash. That was for damn sure.

"Why would you need to use an escort service, Mathew?" Blake asked.

"After my last divorce I decided I wouldn't marry again. And yes, Rafe, I understand that some people have great marriages, but I've been married four times now, and all I got out of each of those marriages was a lighter bank account and some gray hairs — hell, not even a T-shirt. A monumental waste in time and money. My great friend McKenzie Beaumont opened the place, and it's perfect for people who need 'companionship' but don't want anything to do with love."

"Blake, ignore this crap," Rafe said. "We've both been assholes for long enough."

"Believe me, I'm not interested." Blake picked up his drink and took a long swallow.

Mathew wasn't a bit annoyed at their reaction. "Fine. Fine. But I know you, Blake. You'll think about it."

The subject changed, and no further mention was made of needs being met. Still, though the night finished on a good note, Blake found himself feeling restless by the time he arrived home.

And for some odd reason, he pulled the card out of his pocket and placed it on his desk rather than into the wastebasket. But there was no chance in hell he'd call. No need. No interest, even. But out of respect for Mathew, he kept the card. It would soon get lost in the shuffle.

Two weeks later, Blake found himself staring at the simple black writing on the stark white card. He wanted to punch his respected friend in the face for even suggesting an *escort service*. It just wasn't his thing. And yet, somehow, some perverse impulse led him to pick up his phone and dial before he knew what he was doing.

It wasn't that he couldn't get a date. That was never the problem! But this was about having his needs met, his need for control, his need — he had to admit it — for corruption. Relinquish Control's website promised through veiled hints that a man could get any kind of woman he needed.

And right now Blake needed a woman to dominate.

Bound is now available for purchase
at All Major Retailers.

CONTACT MELODY ANNE

Web: www.melodyanne.com

Twitter: @authmelodyanne

Facebook: facebook.com/authormelodyanne

CPSIA information can be obtained at www.ICGtesting.com
Printed in the USA
LVOW04s0009050315

429352LV00030B/566/P